Penguin Books
Death of the Hind Legs and Other Stories

John Wain was born and bred in the Potteries,
and still finds the Midlands the most congenial
area of England. After graduating from Oxford he
spent the next eight years as a university teacher of
English literature, but decided in 1955 that this was
not compatible with an author's life, and gave up
his post, since when he has devoted himself entirely
to writing. He has published, to date, eight novels,
two collections of short stories, four volumes of
poetry, a book on Shakespeare and two volumes of
critical essays. He has more fiction and poetry in
progress, and finds to his dismay that the more
books he writes the more ideas he gets for more
books, so that he has to write faster and faster. He
has not yet hit on a solution to this problem.

Once a considerable traveller, Mr Wain nowadays
prefers to stay quietly at his home in Oxford with
his wife and three sons; his chief recreation is to go
canoeing on the small, slow rivers in which
Oxfordshire is particularly rich.

John Wain's books, *Hurry On Down*, *Nuncle and
Other Stories*, *A Travelling Woman*, and *Strike
the Father Dead* and *The Young Visitors*,
are available as Penguins. His *The Living World of
Shakespeare* is a Pelican.

John Wain

Death of the Hind Legs

and Other Stories

Penguin Books

Penguin Books Ltd, Harmondsworth,
Middlesex, England
Penguin Books Australia Ltd, Ringwood,
Victoria, Australia

This collection first published by Macmillan 1966
Published Penguin Books 1970
Copyright © John Wain, 1963, 1964, 1965, 1966

'King Caliban' first appeared in the *Saturday
Evening Post*, 'A Visit at Tea Time' in *Argosy*,
'Manhood' in *Ladies' Home Journal*, 'Darkness'
in *Harper's Bazaar*, 'The Valentine Generation'
in *Argosy*, 'Further Education' in *Ladies' Home
Journal*, 'Goodnight, Old Daisy' in *Argosy*, 'Down
Our Way' in *The Reporter*, and 'Death of the
Hind Legs' in *Woman's Mirror*.

Made and printed in Great Britain by
Cox & Wyman Ltd, London, Reading and
Fakenham
Set in Linotype Pilgrim

TERRY'S

Contents

King Caliban

Of course, the short explanation is that Fred's always been a bit on the daft side. That's what I said to them straight away, as soon as they began to question me. I'm his brother, I said, and you can take it from me he's never been overburdened with grey matter. I remember that those were the exact words I used. Overburdened with grey matter. Nobody could say Fred was that. But gentle, of course, with all his strength. That's why the whole thing's so ridiculous.

I don't blame them for getting me down there. Just routine. They have to make inquiries. When all's said and done, I was there and saw it happen. So did a thousand other people, of course. But they could hardly have all that lot in. And I was the one he kept talking about. 'You ask Bert,' he kept saying to them. 'Bert'll tell you I didn't mean to do it.' That's what they told me, and I can quite believe it. He always did refer things to me. I used to do the talking for him, even when we were kids, though I was eighteen months younger. Anything Fred couldn't quite explain, send for Bert. I had the brains and he had the brawn. It could have been a good partnership. I say 'could have been', because as things were it never really worked out. If I'd been a type to get into scrapes, to turn people against me and find myself in a position where I needed a big strong brother to stand by me, I'd have found it very convenient to have a giant in the family. But then I wasn't. I always got along all right. I soon learnt to handle people. All you have to do is watch them – keep your eyes open. And I never got into trouble, much, either at school or when I started work. Not real trouble. A bit of boyish high spirits, yes, but to do anything really silly was never in my line. So I just never got into any trouble that I needed pulling out of.

Come to think of it, my quick wits were no more use to him,

really, than his strength and size were to me. I mean to say, I could tell him this and that and the other thing, but I couldn't stop him being stupid. He was slow and that was all there was to it. Of course I always did what I could to help him. Even after we went different ways, or rather I went ahead and he stayed pretty well where he was. For quite long spells we wouldn't see much of each other. But when we did meet, I'd always ask him how he was getting on, and I was always ready to give him a hand where I could. Must do something for Fred, I used to say. Ask anybody. Well, that's how the whole thing came about, isn't it? Me helping him. That's what I said to the police. You try to help somebody, I said, and this is where you land up. In the police-station, being questioned.

If he'd had just a bit more grey matter, none of this would have happened. He'd have got a decent job and earned a decent wage, and then Doreen wouldn't have got on to him so much. Another three quid a week would have satisfied her. It's as simple as that.

All right, I realize you don't know what I'm talking about. Doreen's Fred's wife. They started going together when he first went to work at Greenall's, and they got married quite soon. She was about twenty-nine when he first met her. She was pretty well in charge of the shop. Old Greenall used to call her his right-hand man. Of course she was very wide awake. Knew exactly what they had in stock, whether it was on the shelves or in store, and carried all the prices in her head. Greenall offered to put up her wages, when she said she was leaving. If what I heard at the time was anything to go by, he pretty near offered her double. Said he couldn't do without her. But she just said she'd decided to marry Fred and make a home for him, and she was leaving and that was that. She told him if he could afford to spend that much on wages he could give Fred a bit more, now that he was going to be a breadwinner. But that wouldn't wash, of course. Fred was getting seven pounds already and he wasn't worth more than that of anybody's money.

He was slow, you see. Old Greenall used to say he did a lot of work in a lot of time, and it's true that Fred was never lazy. But he couldn't hold much in his head, he had to keep coming back for instructions, and he could never see for himself the shortest way to do a thing. Greenall used to say that he kept him on because he was as strong as three men and as honest as daylight. And it's true there was a lot of heavy work about the place. There always is, with the grocery. You'd be surprised. Barrels of this and crates of that to be humped about. And loading and unloading the van. Fred used to spend most of his time carrying things about, or doing the deliveries. He hadn't enough grey matter to do any of the paper work, and when they put him on to serving in the shop he was more of a nuisance than anything else, with being so big. The space behind the counter just wasn't wide enough for him. And as for squeezing past him to get at anything, you might as well squeeze past an elephant.

It got on Doreen's nerves from the start. I think she was fond of him in her own way, but between you and me I don't think she'd really thought out all the angles before jumping into holy wedlock. She was pretty scared of being left on the shelf – it's a thought that must come pretty often to a girl who works in a grocery store. She knew what happened when you made a mistake and over-ordered a particular line. You sold what you could, and the rest you got rid of dirt cheap, or, in the end, just chucked it away. That wasn't going to be her. Not little Doreen. As soon as she saw the magic number 30 coming up on the clock, she jumped. And she landed on Fred.

I thought he was rather lucky, at that. She wasn't a bad looker, and she was smart. But she did get on to him about money. She'd saved a bit, and by putting that to what Fred had, they managed to get a house in a decent enough street. But that was just it. They were out of Fred's class, really. Most of the husbands were getting twice what he was getting. So their wives had all sorts of things that Doreen couldn't afford. They managed a telly, but when it came to fridges and cars and stainless steel sinks, and one woman even had a washing-machine! I think it was the washing-machine that put the iron in Doreen's soul. Yes, old Fred wouldn't be in the mess he's in today if it hadn't been for the washing-machine.

One Sunday when I was round there, she really poured out her troubles to me while Fred was out in the garden. The children were with him, skipping round him as he worked and playing some kind of game. They had two, a boy and a girl. They usually stuck with Fred most of the time, when he was home. It always seemed to me that he was fonder of them than she was. Of course in a way I don't blame her. She used to work part time, until they came, so that they weren't so pinched for money. But with two kids to look after, she'd had to give it up. So she had no reason to thank them for coming into the world. Not that she didn't do her best to bring them up right.

Anyway, this Sunday afternoon she stood staring through the window at the three of them. Her face had gone into hard lines and she looked old and miserable. And when she suddenly turned to me, I knew it was coming.

'Bert,' she says, jumping straight in without any messing about, 'can't *you* suggest something?'

'Suggest what kind of something?' I asked.

She looked through the window at Fred and the kids. He was digging trenches, shoving the spade through the wet soil with his great arms as if it was sawdust he was shifting. I never saw anybody as strong as he was. The kids were hanging on to him, shouting something and laughing. I could hear their voices faintly, through the glass.

'What use is he?' said Doreen, following my eyes. 'Tell me that. Here I am, with two kids to bring up and everything to pay for, and what does Fred do?'

'He works,' I said. 'He earns a living, as well as he's able.'

She looked at me, straight in the eyes. 'That's not well enough,' she said. 'You know it and I know it. We all know he's strong, but what's the good of that?'

I looked out at Fred again. He was getting on towards thirty. His body seemed all chest and shoulders. Whether his legs really were very short I don't know, but his great barrel of a torso made them seem like an ape's legs. His hair was beginning to get thin in front. As I watched, he laughed at something one of the children said, and his whole face seemed to go into one enormous smile.

'You be satisfied, that's my advice,' I said to Doreen. 'They don't come any better than old Fred. You'll never be rich, but you've got a good husband and the kids have got a good father.'

'Keep your advice,' she said, 'if that's the best you can do.

Mr Know-it-all. How would you like to live on seven quid, with two children? Scraping for every penny and never having a bit of life. If I want an evening out, the only thing I can afford is to go down to the station and watch the trains come in. He's your brother, and it's not good enough. Who can I turn to, if not you? You've got all the brains, you could easily think of an opening for him. Don't you tell me to be satisfied.' And a lot more like that. Till she got so unpleasant I put my coat on and left.

I tried to forget about Doreen and her troubles. After all, I wasn't her brother, I was Fred's, and he seemed all right. He was quite happy. She nagged him, of course, but what I say is, if you don't want to get nagged, don't get married.

But I couldn't forget her face. She'd suddenly put on twenty years. I mean, she was desperate. And however much I tried to blink it, I had to admit that seven quid was seven quid, for a woman who'd been in a good job and never really gone short. Well, she knew Fred wasn't overburdened with grey matter, I thought to myself. It's her own fault. But that never really works. If you feel sorry for somebody, you can't stop it just by saying it's their own fault. It nags at you. In fact, if you can believe me, it really began to spoil the fun I was getting out of my own life. I was doing pretty well. I'm in building supply, you know. I had a nice little corner in porcelain stuff just then, everything from insulators to wash-basins. I was doing all right, and I'd begun to knock about with a crowd who'd mostly got a fair amount of cash. Chaps who knew their way round. I was on the inside, after always having been on the outside before, and it tasted good. I'd stopped going to the Lord Nelson in the evenings, and taken to looking in at the back bar of the George – the Private Bar. A very nice crowd used to get in there.

Anyway, the reason I mention it is because Len Weather-head used to go there very often. He was really one of the big boys. Savile Row suits, a Bentley, the lot. He'd made it up from the ground and he wasn't fifty yet. Started as some kind of fair-ground attendant, then ran a boxing-booth, and now one of the biggest all-in wrestling promoters in the country ... all-in wrestling! Can't you see how the whole thing seemed to fall smack into my lap?

And yet, funnily enough, I didn't think of it for a week or two. It wasn't until one evening when Len Weatherhead came in looking really brassed off. Dead cheesed. The corners of his mouth were right down and he wasn't speaking to anybody.

Anyway, I generally manage to open people up, and I went to work on him. Pretty soon I had him telling me what was wrong. He couldn't find wrestlers. He'd got the crowds, he'd got the halls, but he couldn't find the boys to wrestle.

'Only today,' he said. 'One of my best pairs. Two boys I could really rely on. Go anywhere, and always put on a good show. Mike the Moose and Billy Crusher, those were their wrestling names. Always put 'em together. Well, all of a sudden Ogden, that's Mike the Moose, comes to me and says he's dissolving the partnership and going to work somewhere as a gym instructor. Says he knows it'll mean a drop in the money, but he prefers the type of work he'll be doing. I ask you! Turning away eighty quid a week!'

'Eighty quid a *week*?' I said. All of a sudden I saw Doreen running to the shop to buy six washing-machines, one for each room.

He nodded. 'In the season,' he said. 'Of course there's not a lot doing between April and September. But those two were a top pair. Always up near the head of the billing. And so well drilled, and accustomed to one another! Knew every wrinkle in the game. Never hurt one another, never had to have any time off with sprains or dislocations or anything like that. And the money I spent on them!'

I began to question him, without letting on that I had anything in my mind except to have an interesting conversation. I learnt a lot in a few minutes. All-in wrestling was something I'd never given any thought to, and I hadn't any idea how it was run. I suppose I just thought it was a matter of a promoter hiring a hall, and then a lot of chaps being entered by their managers, like boxers. But of course all-in isn't a contest, it's a gymnastic display. The wrestlers have to be chaps who know each other and work together. Every fight is rehearsed from beginning to end. You'll notice, if you ever watch a contest, that every time one chap has got the other down and he's putting some fearful lock on him, twisting his limbs about and making him yell blue murder, and you decide he's a goner, the one who's on top suddenly releases his hold and lets him get up. That's because it's his turn to be put through the mill next, till the crowd get tired of it and one of them has to win and make room for another pair.

You'll probably want to ask me what I asked Len Weatherhead. What kind of people watch this? How can they enjoy being treated to this kind of thing, when a child of five could see the fights were rigged? Surely it can't fool them, and if it doesn't fool them, what are they doing there? Len Weatherhead couldn't really answer this and neither can I. In a way, all that happens is that the sight of two big hefty men beating and gouging hell out of one another excites the crowd so much that they don't care whether they're being fooled or not. They don't cool down long enough to be able to think about it one way or the other. They're like middle-aged men watching a striptease. Every one of them knows that the girl isn't taking her clothes off for him, but never mind, he still wants to see her do it.

Len went on to tell me a bit more about how they do it. In some cases, the wrestlers have what you might call characters. The good guy against the bad guy, like Westerns. One of them will wear some costume that makes him look devilish, and have some frightening name like Chang the Terrible or Doctor Death. He'll be fighting some blue-eyed, fair-haired upstanding type, and he'll fight dirty and put the crowd against him. Then they'll scream all sorts of insults at him, and he'll snarl at them and shake his fist, and of course the other chap will let him win right up to the end, and suddenly get the upper hand in the last half-minute and damn near break his neck. That's when they all jump up and down and shout with joy. Look at it this way, where else could they get that amount of fun for half a crown? Football's good value of course, but in football you can't guarantee that the team you support is going to win, and you don't have the fun of seeing the opposing team get kicked and trampled on. That's where all-in definitely scores. It works on some of these feeble-minded types so much that after a season or two of following it, they get to a stage where it's the only sport they *can* follow. Oh yes, somebody had a bright idea there.

'Look here, Len,' I said, choosing a moment when nobody else was likely to come breezing over and listen in. Of course you know what's coming. 'You're really short of wrestlers?' I asked him. 'I mean, if you found a chap who was willing to go in at the bottom of the ladder and who was strong, I mean *really* strong, you'd take him on even if he had no experience?'

He looked a bit crafty at me. 'It would depend,' he said. 'If he had no experience, I'd have to find him a suitable partner and have him trained from the ground up. And he wouldn't be making me a penny during that time. I couldn't afford to keep him on more than part-time, till he was trained.'

We dickered about it a bit and finally he asked me point-blank to come out with whatever it was I had in my mind. So I told him about Fred. A man with the strength of half a dozen wrestlers rolled into one, not making a penny out of it.

Anyway, under his craftiness Len Weatherhead was as keen to do business as I was, and before we drank up and cleared out at closing time I had a nice little deal all buttoned up for Fred. He was to go down to the gym evenings and week-ends, and train with this chap Billy Crusher, who'd been left without a partner. As soon as the training had reached a stage where they could work out a fight and get it rehearsed, they could go on. And when they went on, Fred would move straight into the big money. If he fought three times a week, he'd clear anything from fifty to eighty quid, depending on the gate money.

Of course Len Weatherhead said he'd have to look Fred over first, to see if what I said about him was true, but I knew that wouldn't hold us up. So far from exaggerating about his size and strength, I'd even played it down. I didn't want Len to think of me as a big-mouth. He was a man I could do a lot of business with, if I kept my eyes open and won his confidence. He clapped me on the shoulder before driving off in his Bentley and I felt on top of the world.

Well, there was no point in messing about, so the very next evening I took Fred out for a drink and started to feed the idea into his mind.

'How are the kids, Fred?' I asked him.

'They're coming along fine,' he said. 'I don't know which of them's growing faster. Sometimes I think it's Peter and other times I think it's Paula. They just grow and grow. And *clever*! They get it from their mother, you know. You know what they said the other day?' And he went on to tell me all their clever little sayings. I let him chatter on because I could see it was softening him up. He was doing all the work for me, and all I had to do was listen and buy him a drink now and then.

So I listened until he'd told me everything the kids had done and said since they were one day old, all of which I'd heard before because he never talked about anything else. And when he'd finished I gave the ball another tap to keep it rolling. Money.

'You've got two grand kids,' I said. 'Kids who deserve the best. And there are so many opportunities opening out for youngsters these days. That's where a bit of money comes in handy.'

'That's what Doreen says,' he said, and a look of unhappiness and worry came over his face. Fred's expression never changed quickly, like anyone else's; it seemed to take time for one to fade and another to take its place. Like sand castles being washed out by the tide. I suppose that was the slowness of his mind.

I knew there was no prospect of rushing him too fast, what with the time it took him to get hold of an idea, so I decided to jump straight in. I asked him if he'd ever heard of Len Weatherhead. He hadn't. I told him Len Weatherhead made a lot of money, for himself and everybody else, by promoting all-in wrestling. Fred thought for a bit and I half expected him to ask me what all-in wrestling was, but finally he must have decided that he'd heard of it, so he turned his head slowly towards me and said, 'Yes?'

'Yes,' I said. 'And what's more, Len Weatherhead is very interested in you, Fred. Very interested indeed.'

'Interested in me?' he said, tapping himself on the chest to make quite sure we had our identities sorted out.

'Yes, you,' I said. 'He's heard all about you as a big strong muscle-man. That's the main thing, you know, in the wrestling game. The rest can be learnt. They have a gym where they train you.'

It was as plain as a pikestaff that he simply didn't know what I was getting at. All-in wrestling, and gym, and training just weren't anything to do with him; that was that. I felt irritated suddenly. I wanted to drag him along. Cut through that slowness of his.

'Listen, Fred,' I said. 'Why do you think I'm bothering to tell you this?'

'Is it a bother?' he said. 'I thought we were just having a pint together.'

'Well, so we are,' I said. After all he was my brother. 'But you're lucky, Fred. You've got a smart brother who keeps his eyes open for you.'

'Well, thanks,' he said.

'I can put you in the money,' I said, rushing it along. 'No more trouble with Doreen. Everything you want for the kids. Dress them up lovely. Take them on holidays. Send them to a nice school.'

'You can do this?' he asked, looking at me with his eyes wide open. I knew I'd hit the right note.

'Just play along with me,' I said, clapping him on the shoulder, 'and I can put you in a position to make eighty quid a week.'

At that, he burst out laughing. Or rather, laughter slowly welled up out of that big chest of his. It took about two minutes to get from his belly as far as his voice.

'All right, laugh,' I said. 'But when you've finished laughing, let me put you in the picture. Eighty quid sounds a lot to you. It even sounds a lot to me. But it's just everyday stuff to Len Weatherhead.'

Fred searched in his memory for the name Len Weatherhead, which he'd heard about two minutes before, and finally he lifted his head in that perplexed way of his, looked at me and said: 'Wrestling?'

'Wrestling,' I said. 'Just the job you were cut out for.'

He picked up his beer as if he was going to take a swig at it, but he only looked at it and then put it down and faced me again.

'You're joking, Bert,' he said. 'It's one of your jokes.'

'Eighty quid a week,' I said. 'Don't believe me. Don't listen to me. Go and see Len Weatherhead.'

He shook his head.

'Now look, Fred,' I said. 'Do you want to have nice things for Peter and Paula or don't you?'

'They're all right,' he said, almost fiercely. 'They don't go short. I take care of them and we have good times together. They've got a house to live in and a garden –'

'And they could have so much more,' I cut in, quickly, 'if their father would just realize his own potentialities.'

That last word threw him, naturally. It was the sort of word you hear chucked about in the Private Bar in the George, but not in the Lord Nelson, where we were.

'Don't mess me about, Bert,' he said. 'Don't mess me about with long words. I do a job and the wage comes in and we live on it. We can be happy.'

I didn't want to get stuck on that point, so I just pushed along. First I drew a picture of Doreen's sufferings, then I looked forward to the time when the kids were teenagers and needed all sorts of things to help them keep up with the crowd – smart clothes and motor-scooters and the rest of it. I told him it wouldn't always be enough for them to play with him in the garden.

'You're doing all right,' I said, '*now*. But wait till they get bigger. You'll need four, five times the money you're making now. Who's going to give it to you? Greenall? That's a laugh and you know it.'

I got him so worried that finally he agreed to come with me and see Len Weatherhead. But first I thought I'd better take him to a wrestling bout, to give him an idea of what he was going into. I didn't want Len Weatherhead to write him off as a total nitwit the first time he met him. He had to be in the picture somewhere.

So a couple of nights later we went down to the Town Hall for one of Len's promotions. It was the usual thing – tickets from about half a crown to a quid, the place pretty well packed out, and everybody excited at the prospect of seeing some licensed mayhem.

Right from the start I knew I was going to have trouble with Fred. I'd taken a lot of trouble to get him into a nice relaxed mood, so much trouble that I really wondered, now and then, why I was doing it. Just brotherly love, was all I could think of. I'd called at his house and picked him up by car – with Doreen's full approval, of course, because I'd told her what I was doing –

and on the way down I'd stopped and got a couple of drinks inside him and even stood him a cigar, one of those one-and-ninepenny Panatellas that people like Fred associate with Christmas.

But it was no good. Even before the first pair of wrestlers came out, I could see that he didn't like it. The atmosphere upset him. There was a kind of edge to it that upset him. Of course he was always so gentle, he hated any kind of upset or violence. As we sat there waiting, I looked round at the scene and for a moment I saw it through his eyes. There was the huge hall, dimly lit, with clouds of cigarette-smoke drifting up to the ceiling. And the ring, with all that white light beating down on it, like an operating table all ready for someone's guts to be cut out. And the faces of the people sitting round us weren't too pleasant, some of them. Probably you wouldn't have minded them in a crowd, but here they seemed more ugly and cruel, with the sort of thoughts that were going on in their minds.

Then I thought, *eighty quid a week*! And I knew I'd talk Fred into it, with Doreen's help, whatever he thought about this evening.

Well, it started, and I must say I hardly saw anything of the programme. I was too busy hanging on to Fred, trying to calm him down and make him stay in his seat. If I hadn't been there I don't think he'd have stayed beyond the first minute of the first bout. There was all the usual razzmatazz, the M.C. coming out and shouting the names, and then the ref. and the two fighters going into a huddle. One called Eskimo Jim and the other Paddy Doyle, or some such name. Eskimo Jim was the bad one. You could see at once he was going to fight dirty. He didn't look much like a real Eskimo, but he had thick lips and a flat nose and his eyes were sort of slanted. The Irish chap was good-looking, of course. It was the most obvious bit of pairing-off you could imagine. All the time the ref. was briefing them, or pretending to, the crowd were barracking Eskimo Jim and he was glaring murder at them, but the ref. pulled him back, of course. And all the time Paddy stood looking calm and handsome. I'd have laughed if I hadn't been so worried about the way Fred was taking it. He didn't seem to see the funny side at all. The insults and the shouting, and the fist-shaking and threats, were all having a terrible effect on him. It was like trying to lead a horse past something it's afraid of. 'Relax, Fred, relax,' I kept saying to him. 'It's just entertainment, see? It's not a fight – it's an acrobatic performance. Remember that – just an acrobatic performance.' And just as I said the words, Eskimo Jim pushed the referee to one side and started to fight before Paddy was ready. Of course. He jumped at him, grabbed his head, and swung it down to knee-level, twisting it at the same time so that he damn near dragged it off. Then, while Paddy was reeling about all dazed, he gave him a kick in the guts that you could hear all over the building. It was very clever, really, the way they managed it. But it was too much for Fred. He was out of his seat in an instant, and if we hadn't been sitting in the middle of a row he'd have been half-way down the aisle and I'd never have got him back. It was the other customers who saved the situation for me. They'd paid for their seats, the butchery had only just begun and they didn't want their view blocked right away by this big elk of a man pushing past them. They turned and hissed at him to sit down, and he did. But he wouldn't look at the ring.

Well, we stuck it out. About half-way through the evening, Fred seemed to slump in his seat, as if the will to resist had left him, and he didn't try to get away any more. Just sat there staring straight in front of him. I couldn't even decide, when I glanced at him, whether he was watching the wrestlers or not. As for me, I settled down and watched the show. After all, I'd paid for it. And if Fred wasn't concentrating, then I'd got to watch hard enough for two. I don't like to waste my money.

We went across to the pub afterwards and I lined up a couple of refreshing pints. Fred threw his down in about four swallows. I could see his hand trembling as he lifted the glass. There was no need to ask him what he thought about all-in wrestling.

'Well, that's it, Fred. 'I said. 'I'm not going to try to talk you into anything. I've lined up a chance for you, and if you don't want to take it, that's your affair.'

He turned and looked at me. His face was dead white: I'd never seen it like that before. 'You mean you still want me to go in for *that*?' he asked. I didn't answer, and he didn't say anything more. I finished my pint and then I drove him home. Well, I was thinking to myself, that's one more thing that's no good.

Doreen was waiting for us when we got back to the house. I was feeling pretty savage about wasting all that time and money, and when she asked me to come in for a cup of tea, I said *no*. In fact I didn't even get out of the car. She called to me from the doorway and when she saw I wasn't going to move, she came down to the gate and spoke to me through the car window.

'What's wrong?' she asked in her direct way.

'Oh, nothing,' I said. 'Fred doesn't like all-in wrestling, that's all. We'll have to think of some other spare-time hobby for him.'

And I drove off. Let him sort it out, I thought. I could imagine him trying to explain to Doreen that he didn't want to go in for wrestling even if it did mean eighty quid a week. And, being in a savage mood, I felt it served him right. I'd had a lot of trouble and expense, and what was worse, I was going to look a big-mouth when I next talked to Len Weatherhead. Just a stupid, unreliable big-mouth. Let her put him through it, I thought as I locked up the garage.

After that, I just assumed it was all over. I kept away from the George for the next few evenings, beccause I wouldn't have known what to say to Len Weatherhead if I'd met him. I thought I'd let the idea just get lost of its own accord. Anyway, it was a good thing I didn't rush into any big explanation with Len, because the next thing that happened was something that really surprised me.

I was sitting in the office one morning. I call it the office, though it's only one room and I still do all my own secretarial work. But that won't last. I've got my eye on a bigger place already, and business is looking up all the time. Anyway, I was sitting there, working out a bit of costing on some wash-hand basins, when the door opened – there was Fred. In the middle of the morning, I ask you.

'What's up?' I said. 'Got the sack?'

'I'm on deliveries,' he said. 'I just wanted to look in and have a word with you.'

'What about?' I said. Rather cool. I wasn't in a mood to let him forget that he'd disappointed me.

'Look,' he said, coming all the way into the room, but not sitting down. 'This Len Who'sit. When can you take me to him?'

I looked up into his face and all of a sudden I saw what must have happened. He looked like somebody who'd just been repatriated from Devil's Island.

'Been talking things over with Doreen, have you?' I asked him, keeping it as casual as I could.

'When can I see this Len?' he asked, ignoring my question. Of course he wouldn't want to talk about it. Doreen must have really turned it loose on him, to drive him to the state where he'd rather go into the ring with Eskimo Jim than face her in his own house.

I reached for the telephone and dialled Len Weatherhead's office number. I wasn't going to let this go cool. Too much depended on it. The luck was with me: he was in and I got hold of him straight away. Before I hung up I had it all fixed for Fred to go and see him and talk business.

After that, I relaxed. I knew that Fred wouldn't change his mind. He might change his mind about wanting to be a wrestler, but he wouldn't go back on his arrangement to see Len Weatherhead. Which made it Weatherhead's job to talk him into it. All I had to do was to sit back and collect thanks and smiles all round.

The next few days passed very smoothly. I largely by-passed Fred and got the score from Doreen. She welcomed me, now, as nice as pie. I was the life-saver who had turned her grocer's-assistant husband into a big, rich wrestler. At least he was headed that way. Len had evidently taken to him and seen how far his strength would take him in the wrestling business, because he'd given him the full treatment. Taken him all round the gym and everything. If Fred still wanted to back out, he didn't get a chance to, because the next thing Len did was to arrange for him to meet Billy Crusher. That's the fellow who was in partnership with Mike the Moose, who'd now gone legit. as a gym instructor.

I suppose Billy did more than anyone to talk Fred into the

game. He had a professional attitude, which was all the more refreshing because he was going to be with Fred, right there in the ring. He wasn't asking Fred to do anything he wasn't going to do himself. That put him straight away in a different class from me, Doreen, Len Weatherhead, and the crowd. I heard so much about Billy Crusher, whose name was really Arthur Trubshaw, that one Sunday morning I looked in, out of curiosity, to watch the pair of them training at Weatherhead's gym.

They were already at it when I arrived, so I stood back and watched them. Arthur was a big, powerful chap, but even so he wasn't as strong as Fred. He was much faster and lighter on his feet, with being a trained acrobat and all that, and I could see that he was watching Fred very carefully. He wasn't exactly afraid of him, but he was being very wary. He didn't want any mistakes, because he knew that if Fred should happen to forget the script and let loose that strength of his in the wrong direction, there was every chance of getting hurt. And he wasn't in the business to get hurt, I could see that. He was a clever performer, almost flashy. He knew exactly what he was doing. And his face was unmarked. Nobody had ever taken a swipe at him and broken his nose, and they weren't going to if he could help it.

When I got there, he was showing Fred the way to get out of a lock. The drill was that Arthur got Fred on his back and twisted his legs round in a way that looked bloody agonizing to me, but (as I heard Arthur keep telling Fred) wouldn't do him any harm as long as he was expecting it and relaxed. They were to hold this for a bit, while Fred was supposed to writhe about in agony, and then all of a sudden Fred was to draw his knees up and kick out, so that his feet caught Arthur full in the chest and threw him backwards. Then they could go on to the next move. Arthur was pointing out to Fred, very carefully, the exact point on his chest where the feet were to land. No messing about. He didn't want a kick under the heart to make him feel groggy, and neither on the other hand did he want either of the feet to go too high up and get him in the throat. He indicated an exact area and he rehearsed the thing till Fred could have done it in his sleep. Never an inch too high or too low. I was just leaning against the wall, having a smoke and watching the fun, when I heard Len Weatherhead's voice in my ear. 'Seem to be getting to know each other all right,' he said.

'That chap Arthur'll bring Fred along all right,' I said. 'He's working very hard on him.'

'I should hope he is working hard,' said Len, a bit sourly. 'He's on full pay during this training period and he doesn't have to fight any bouts. He gets as much for one of these training sessions as he does for a fight in the ring.'

Just as he spoke, Fred brought his fist down in the small of Arthur's back. Arthur must have told him to, but perhaps Fred was an inch or two outside the target area, or brought it down too hard, or something. Anyway, Arthur collapsed on the floor, gasping that his kidneys were ruptured and that he was going straight off to his lawyer to sue everybody all round. Fred stood over him, looking apologetic, and Len Weatherhead went over to try to soothe him.

'Bad luck, Arthur,' he said, trying to pass it off all cheerful. 'Fred'll have to watch what he's doing, won't you, Fred?'

'It looks easy from where you're standing,' said Arthur, fixing Len Weatherhead with a very cold eye. His face was white. 'I ought to get double pay for this,' he said.

'Oh, come on, Arthur,' said Len, fencing him off. 'You know you do all right.'

'All right, is it?' said Arthur, climbing to his feet. 'You come and have a bash at it if it's all right.'

'What did I do wrong?' Fred puts in, as if he was back at Greenalls and had put some bags of flour in the wrong place or something.

'I'll show you what you did wrong,' said Arthur suddenly, and without warning he seized hold of the back of Fred's neck, dragged his head down till he was bent double, and then slammed him in the kidneys with his fist. It made me feel faint to see it. As for Fred, he crumpled up. I thought he was going to be sick. Finally he dragged himself on to his hands and knees, but he couldn't get any further.

'That's what I'm talking about,' said Arthur. Really cool he was. 'Get that into your head and maybe we'll start making progress.'

'Fred,' I said through the ropes. 'How are you feeling?'

'Don't overdo it, Arthur,' said Len Weatherhead.

'He's got to learn,' said Arthur. But he sounded a bit nervous, because Fred was climbing to his feet now, with sweat breaking out all over his face, and he didn't like the look in his eyes. None of us did. All his gentleness was gone and his face seemed full of nothing but pain and rage. As I'd noticed before, his huge chest made him seem top-heavy, and as he took a step or two towards Arthur, he seemed to waddle like a gorilla.

Arthur stood his ground, but I noticed that he fell automatically into a wrestler's crouch, ready to defend himself. He sank his head down between his shoulders so that he wouldn't get his neck broken. Just instinct, I suppose. Actually it was all over in a couple of seconds. Len and I both broke into action. He climbed through the ropes and got between them, and at the same time I leaned over and got hold of Fred's arm.

'Don't do it, Fred,' I said. 'It's me, Bert.'

He hadn't realized I was there, and the sound of my voice started him out of his trance. But his mind moved slowly, as usual, and it was like watching a diver come up from the ocean floor.

'He hit me,' Fred said to me, as if we were back on the old asphalt playground.

'That's enough for today. Out of the ring,' said Len Weatherhead in his manager's voice.

Arthur came over to Fred and looked him straight in the eye. I had to admire his pluck.

'No offence, Fred,' he said. 'I got a bit rattled when you hit me in the wrong place, that's all. Let's try that again.'

I liked him for doing it his own way, ignoring Len Weatherhead's order to break it up for the day. And he was certainly risking something by inviting Fred to give him another punch. But it worked perfectly. They went through three or four movements that looked for all the world like dance steps, and then Fred swung his fist down, and this time it must have been placed right, because although the sound thumped out like somebody kicking a suitcase, Arthur just grinned, and the two of them went off to get dressed.

As I turned away I saw Len Weatherhead staring after them,

looking very excited. 'I've got a name for him,' he said. 'Did you see that look that came over his face? Sort of ape-like? That's worth a fortune in the ring.'

Well, a fortune was a fortune, but Fred was still my brother, so I didn't exactly gush over this discovery of his. 'What's the name?' I said, a bit short.

'King Caliban,' he said.

'King Who?' I asked. It sounded a bit funny to me.

'Caliban. He was some kind of monster on a desert island, as far as I know. That's the angle to stress, for Fred. The barbaric.'

'Why not call him the Missing Link and have done with it?' I asked. But as soon as I'd spoken I wished I hadn't. I could see I'd pushed it too far. If I wanted to stay in with Len, I had to leave him to run his business his own way. He gave me a look that told me pretty clearly that when he wanted my advice he'd ask me for it. So of course I decided to belt up and make myself scarce. I didn't want to spoil everything now that it seemed set fair. I mean to say, it's through playing along with chaps like Len Weatherhead that chaps like me get their place in the sun.

After that, I played it cool for a while. I kept my nose out of it and didn't see anything of Len, or Fred and Doreen, for that matter. Time jogged along and I knew it must be time for Fred and Arthur to have a bout in public, but I didn't think about it much. Then, late one afternoon as I was just locking up the office, Doreen showed up.

'I want you to do me a favour, Bert,' she said, coming to the point as usual.

'I know,' I said. 'Hold Fred's hand when he goes into the ring.'

'No, be serious,' she said, giving me a very worried look. Her face had gone thin, it seemed to me. Something had frightened her.

'Fred's acting up strange,' she said. 'Since he gave up Green-all's and gave all his time to practising with Arthur.'

'I didn't even know he'd done that,' I said.

'Yes, the last three weeks before their first bout,' she said. 'That was the arrangement. The three weeks'll be up in four days. Mr Weatherhead's been paying him the same wage as

27

he'd have got at Greenall's. Then as soon as he starts having professional fights he'll get the same pay as Arthur.'

So he hadn't started to touch the big money yet. Just the worry and the uncertainty.

'Where do I come in?' I asked her.

'Fred doesn't like it,' she said. 'He's doing it for everybody's sake, but he doesn't like it. And sometimes he seems so strange. I hardly feel I know him any more.'

'When he's earning you eighty quid a week,' I said, 'you won't care whether you know him or not.'

'Bert, that's not fair,' she said and all of a sudden if she didn't burst out crying. Doreen of all women!

'He frightens me,' she said, sobbing so you could hear her in the street. 'The other day we had a bit of a difference about the children. I was for telling them about his new job and he said no, let them think he still worked at Greenall's. But they're bound to find out, Fred, I said to him, why not tell them now? Besides, Peter'll be so proud to have a real wrestler for his dad. I was going on like that when all of a sudden he gave a sort of roar. I never heard him make a noise like that before. And he glared at me. His eyes seemed like an animal's. Christ, Bert, I can't explain it. I thought he was going to murder me.'

'Did he lay a finger on you?' I asked.

'No,' she said.

'Well, then,' I said. 'If every man who shouted at his wife could scare her as much as you're scared, the world'd be a happier place.'

She seemed a bit easier in her mind. After all, there's nothing like having somebody tell you your fears are just imagination. But she hadn't finished with me. She pressed on to the next point.

'Promise you'll come to the fight on Tuesday night, Bert,' she said. 'I feel I must be there, but I can't stand it by myself.'

'Why don't you stay at home?' I said.

'Oh, I couldn't,' she said. 'I must be with him.'

It seemed a funny idea to me. With him. Her and a thousand other people. But I said I'd go. I wasn't keen, but she was anxious and besides, I was curious to see how the act would go over.

I asked Doreen if she'd got any free tickets, and she said no. Somehow, that riveted it. I mean it really convinced me that she *must* be feeling bad about things, to overlook a chance of saving at least fifteen bob.

Anyway, I called for her on the night. She'd asked me to go round at about six, to have a bit of a meal before we set off, and as luck would have it I got there just as Fred was leaving. Len Weatherhead, giving him the V.I.P. treatment, because it was his first bout, had called for him in his Bentley, and Arthur was along too. The three of them were just coming out of the house as I got there, and I must say it looked exactly like a man being arrested by two Scotland Yard detectives. They were jollying him along, and Arthur was even carrying the little suitcase which – I suppose – contained his wrestling outfit. I recognized it. It was his old football case. He used to keep his shorts and boots and things in it, with a little bottle of embrocation. That was when we were between eighteen and twenty-one, both living at home. It made me feel funny to see the old football case going out through the door, on such different business. And there was old Fred. He didn't recognize me. At least, I spoke to him and he looked at me, but he seemed to stare straight through me. His face looked sad and lonely. Yes, *lonely*, as if he'd spent about five years in a desert and given up hope of ever meeting another human being.

Well, I thought, the first time is always uphill, whatever it is you're doing. He'll settle down. I went on into the house and there was Doreen with the children. She'd got some sort of game out on the table, a jigsaw or something and was trying to get them interested in it, to cover up for Fred. But she wasn't having much luck. They could tell there was something going on, and they both kept asking where Dad was till it nearly drove her nuts.

We ate some kippers, neither of us saying anything much, and then the neighbour who was going to mind the kids came in and we got into our coats and on our way. In the car I started trying to raise Doreen's spirits a bit. 'As of tonight,' I said to her, 'you and Fred can kiss your worries good-bye. A solid fifty to eighty quid a week in the season, and he can always go back to humping groceries when his reactions begin to slow down and he can't wrestle any longer. You're a very lucky girl,' I told her.

'But if it's going to make Fred different,' she whined, but I cut her short. I wasn't having any of that. 'Different my foot,' I said. 'It's just exchanging one trade for another that's a bit worrying at first. This isn't fighting. It's an acrobatic display, and Fred's been well trained for it. It's the chance of a lifetime. Considering he isn't overburdened with grey matter, this kind of thing is the only kind of work he can be trained for.'

She quietened down a bit, but when we got to the Town Hall and saw the crowd streaming in, she got all upset again, and to tell the truth I didn't feel any too good myself. The faces! They seemed like things you'd see in a nightmare. I didn't know which were the worst, the men or the women. There were women of all ages, from old grandmothers down to teenagers, and they all had that bright-eyed look that people wear when they're going to see something really horrible. *To see a man get beaten up and hurt* – that was what they were there for, and it was as plain as if they'd had it on sandwich boards. Perhaps they'd all been ill treated by a man at some time or other. Perhaps every woman has. Well, I thought, at least the all-in game is one that won't lack support. The cinemas can close, the dog-tracks can close, but this'll keep going. Fred's on to a good thing, I told myself. But I wasn't too happy inside.

The usual flourishing and announcing went on, and then the first bout started. It was between a character covered from head to foot in red tights, with just little holes for his eyes, and another chap who'd gone to the other extreme and was nearly naked. The red one was called the Scarlet Fiend or the Red Devil or something. He was the one the crowd were supposed to be against, though as far as I could see they were both equally horrible and when it came to fighting dirty, hitting the other chap when he wasn't looking and the rest of it, there was nothing to choose. But the crowd were there for thrills, and they started to get worked up straight away. The girls! screaming advice, too. Where they picked it up I don't know. But the worst was a big bald-headed fellow about four seats away from me. We were in the third row from the ringside, and I could see that if they'd been ringside seats this chap would have had his head through the ropes to shout at the wrestlers better. He seemed completely beside himself. He wanted to see murder committed. Nothing short of complete bestiality would satisfy him. He must have been some kind of pervert like you read about in the Sunday paper. He never stopped shouting from the first minute to the last. And when the action really got hot, he'd leap to his feet and start dancing about with excitement, till the people behind him had to grab him and pull him down again, so they could see.

I saw Doreen glancing at this bald chap once or twice, and I could tell what she was thinking. If he shouted like that when Fred was fighting, she wasn't going to be able to stand it. I made a little joke about him, trying to get her to see him as funny, but I couldn't put my heart into it. I didn't think he was funny myself, that was the trouble. So I concentrated on the money. 'It's worth it for eighty quid,' I said to Doreen. She gave me an expressionless look and I couldn't tell what was going on in her mind.

We watched three or four more bouts and I began to feel numb. My sense of proportion came back and I thought, well, it's just a lot of silly fools shouting and getting worked up. 'All in the day's work,' I said to Doreen. She gave me the same look again.

I got so sunk in my thoughts that I hardly watched the ring any more, and it shook me to hear all of a sudden the name 'Billy Crusher' shouted out by the M.C. He went on to tell the fans that this popular fighter was back after a spell of rest and that he was matched tonight with the most dangerous opponent he had ever faced, a new import never before seen in any ring in the civilized world, an untamed giant straight from the jungle. And there they were climbing into the ring, and the M.C. was bawling, 'KING CALIBAN!'

As soon as I saw the two of them up there I knew how it was going to be slanted. Arthur had those flashy good looks, especially when you saw him from a few yards away, with the arc lights shining down on that smooth torso of his. The idol of the gallery. Especially the women. Fred, by contrast, would have looked pretty lumpy and plain anyway, and to make it worse they'd dressed him in a leopard skin so that he looked like a jungle chieftain in a B picture. I don't think they'd actually used grease-paint on him, but it's a fact that his face looked much uglier than I'd ever seen it before. Perhaps it was just the angle at which I was looking up at him, but his forehead seemed narrow and sloping. I don't think I'd have recognized him if I hadn't known.

The crowd were well away by now, having witnessed half a dozen crimes of violence already, and they started barracking poor old Fred straight away, calling him all sorts of names, and telling Arthur to throttle him and put a stop to his career. I knew Fred was supposed to feed all this by reacting and making all sorts of threatening gestures, but he just stood there looking lonely, as if he was still wandering in that solitary desert. It made him seem sub-human, like a bear that had been brought in to be baited. I glanced at Doreen. She had her head bent and was staring down at her feet. I knew she wouldn't look at the ring.

The fight started and they went pretty smoothly into the routine. Arthur's training had been good, and I was hoping they'd get through without any accidents and finish with it, so that I could take Doreen home. Then when she had Fred back with her, plus a big fat pay-packet, things would seem rosier. This was the low ebb, having to sit there and watch them twist one another's limbs.

The bald chap seemed to have taken a real dislike to Fred, and he was hooting insults at him right from the start, rejoicing whenever Arthur looked like maiming him, and groaning like a stuck pig when Fred was on top. I nearly leaned over and asked him to shut up, but it wouldn't have done any good. He was demented. I think he wanted to attract Fred's attention, to have him come to the ropes and shake his fist or threaten to come down and do him. That's what those nut cases want – to be in on the act. 'Serve you right!' he'd scream, whenever Fred got jumped on or twisted. 'That's what you need!' I could see it was making Doreen sick, and I felt a bit dicky myself.

What was worse, I could see that Baldy was beginning to rattle Fred. His voice was very penetrating, and it must have got in through Fred's insulation, so to speak. Every time he was taking punishment, to hear that screech right in his ear – it was enough to send him round the bend, if he hadn't been half-way there already.

At one point, after they'd done a very clever double fall which ended with Fred being thrown up in the air and landing on his back, Baldy set up such a howl of glee that Fred turned on one elbow and looked at him. He could see who was doing the shouting, and he gave him the same look that I'd seen him give Arthur in the gym that morning. His sub-human look. I felt myself break into a sweat. If that was how he'd looked at Doreen no wonder she was frightened. He slowly got to his feet, still glaring at Baldy, then slowly he turned to face Arthur, who was waiting to get on with the act.

From that moment on, Fred's performance went to pieces. His timing went off and he seemed to be acting in a dream. He was so much slower than Arthur that Arthur had to keep waiting for him, and it began to look obvious. I saw Arthur's lips moving and I could see he was whispering to Fred, trying to get him to snap it up. Then, suddenly, Fred made a bad mistake. He put the wrong lock on Arthur and really hurt him. Arthur twisted away, and with the same quick flash of temper as I'd seen him show before, he dug his elbow savagely into Fred's ribs. It was more petulant than anything else – a kind of reminder to keep his mind on the job. But it was too much. Fred must have seen red. He swung round and slapped Arthur across the side of the head with his open hand. It made him reel across the ring. And before anyone could stop them, they were fighting. It was the strangest thing I ever saw, the way they switched from mock fighting to real in a couple of seconds. They were both mad and out to hurt each other.

Naturally that didn't last long. The ref. saw what was going on, and moved in to break it up. But at that moment Arthur got a punch in that went under Fred's ribs and made him gasp for breath. He stood there for a moment, fighting for breath, and at that moment I saw his face. It was quite calm, just very lonely. As if he'd gone beyond anyone's power to help him or speak to him.

It was all over in a moment. Fred pushed the ref. away, turned to Arthur and suddenly swung a fist in the air, like a club, then crashed it down on Arthur's skull. The whole place fell silent. Everybody knew this was not fooling. Arthur lurched, tried to put his hands up to his head, then fell forward. I remember thinking, 'He's killed him.' I still don't know, for that matter. He's still unconscious but he may get better.

I told you a lie. I said the whole place fell silent. But there was one still on his feet and shouting. Yes. The bald chap. He was pointing a finger straight at Fred and screaming, 'Dirty! A foul! He fouled him!' Nobody else was moving or making a sound, but Baldy couldn't stop yelling. I suppose he was hysterical.

Then, like a nightmare, I saw Fred come across the ring and through the ropes. I tried to call him, but my throat was dry and nothing came out. I knew at once what he was going to do. The people on the front row scattered as he walked straight over them. And the second row. The ref. jumped down and tried to scramble after him. Doreen was screaming. But it was too late, he'd got hold of the bald chap and was lifting him above his head like a log of wood. Higher and higher he lifted him. My voice came back and I cried, 'Don't do it, Fred! Don't do it!'

But he did it. He flung the man down across the wooden seats, as if it was the seats he hated and he was using the man's body to break them with.

Don't ask me how we got out of there. Of course the police were there within five minutes. They got Fred into a Black Maria even before they got the bald chap into an ambulance. As far as I can make out, he'll live. So it all might have been worse. Of course I feel a bit shaken. I spent the night on the settee at Doreen's, after the police let me go. But I didn't sleep. And I haven't felt up to doing anything all day. As I said to them, that's what happens when you try to help anybody. Well, it's a lesson to me. Let them get on with it from now on.

Doreen's telephoned to say that Fred's been asking for me. Well, let him ask. He got himself into this, let him get himself out. I mean to say, all right, it was my idea for him to go in for wrestling. But how was I to know he'd do a bloody silly thing like that?

And what am I going to say to Len Weatherhead when I meet him?

Come In, Captain Grindle

By three o'clock the afternoon silence was so heavy with anxiety that Laura Daniel was relieved, as well as startled and disquieted, by the sudden hectoring summons of the telephone. As she moved across the room to answer it, a shaft of hot sunlight fell across her body. Outside, the trees in the quiet street nodded gaily. She thought, as she had thought ten thousand times before, of the gulf that severed her outer from her inner life. Comfort, dignity, even beauty on the outside: tension, fear, anguish within.

'Laura? Good news, darling. I've got everything fixed.'

Thank you, Edna, and may a silent curse eat the marrow from your trim young bones.

'Everybody's really discreet at the agency. I had a word with the man who'll be . . . doing the job. He was obviously as reliable as a sheepdog.'

Did he growl? Did he bark much? Did he make short rushes to and fro?

'It's all arranged, darling. All you have to do is ring the number I gave you and tell them when you want the man to come and see you.'

'Edna, I want to – '

'Mr Grindle, his name is. No, wait a minute, *Captain* Grindle. Isn't that sweet? It goes with his manner. He's all stiff back and military bearing. Captain Grindle. You can have absolutely perfect confidence in – '

'Edna. I don't want to go on with it.'

There was a pause, and when Edna Marchant's voice resumed, it had a new hardness.

'Laura, are we going to have all *that* again? You told me on Monday that you'd decided *definitely* – '

Laura Daniel's heart thumped. She wanted to bang the

receiver back into its rest, but she was too afraid of the silence that would follow. As long as Edna went on talking, she could still tell herself that something was being done, that she was not just drifting through a tunnel of unhappiness that had no ending. Yes, Edna must go on talking. But she must resist, at the same time. Edna must not push her into this horror. She must reach out, grab something and cling.

'Edna, I know you want to help me, but it's – you must see it from my point of view.'

'But *darling* Laura, we've been into all that so many times. It's precisely because I'm outside the situation that I'm able to – '

'Yes, my dear, I know. But you don't have to run the risks. I have to run them and I can't bear it. I'm too frightened.'

'What of? A show-down?'

Laura Daniel took a deep breath which made her aware, suddenly, of the scent of a delicate bunch of freesias on the bookcase beside the telephone. A gift from Bernard. His lavishness with small attentions, his never entering the house without a small gift for her, was the infallible mark of a successful affair. On his way home from the current love-nest, some impulse never failed to drive him to a flower-stall, a shop for chocolates or perfume, even – if he were feeling particularly buoyant – a jeweller's. She glanced at the bracelet on her frail wrist. What wanderings in a landscape of pleasure, what heights and divings unknown to her, unguessable by her, must it represent? As the thought crossed her mind, she braced herself for a rush of resentment. But nothing came, nothing, she felt nothing.

'I can't face it, Edna,' she said into the indifferent mouthpiece. 'If I set detectives on Bernard, sooner or later he'll leave me. He's always tried to keep his infidelities a secret from me, and that in itself is a sign that he wants our marriage to go on.'

'But surely that's just what you were complaining about. You told me it was being lied to that really hurt you.'

'It does hurt me.'

'Then darling, why don't you follow the plan we hit on? Confront him with the complete evidence, let him understand that you know *everything*, and then you can afford to be very sweet and generous and let the shock bring him to his senses.'

His senses? How can I control his senses? Aloud she said, 'I know, Edna, it looks like the most practical idea on the surface, but – '

'Well, it's what I'd do, I can tell you. If I had any woman trouble with James.'

Laura Daniel had a sudden vision of Edna's husband, James. He seemed to be standing in front of her, in the middle of the patch of sunlight on the carpet, his puffy eyes seeking hers with an expression of good-natured bewilderment. Edna was younger than she but James was older than Bernard. Edna had the confidence and briskness of a woman not yet haunted by her future. She was not yet thirty-five. The years stretched ahead for her with a placid spaciousness that promised to forgive mistakes. But for her, Laura, the future was a narrowing path towards a dead end of loneliness. 'Woman trouble' with James! One could as easily imagine James shooting Niagara in a barrel as approaching a new woman and making amorous demands of her.

'Edna, I'm sure your plan would work very well with James, but Bernard's – '

'Why do you call it my plan? It's *our* plan, isn't it? We worked it out step by step together on Monday, and all I've been doing since is to take some of the running about and organizing off your hands.'

Laura had a sudden, grotesque picture of herself running about on her hands, feet kicking uselessly in the air. 'Yes, I know, dear, and it's very good of you,' she said feebly. 'But you know how apt one is to distrust one's first thoughts in a business like this.'

'I don't,' came Edna's quick, serious voice. 'If one thinks one's first thoughts carefully enough, and slowly enough, they're firm. And all one has to do then is to stand firmly by them.'

Laura Daniel had been standing; now she sank limply into a chair, as if Edna's insistence had physically overpowered her, pushed her down into subservience.

'Listen, darling, I was unhinged on Monday. I mean, I'd tried to keep all this unhappiness sewn up inside me, to carry it about and never let anyone catch a glimpse of it, and suddenly – it

37

just – ' She caught herself gesturing helplessly with the hand that was not holding the telephone.

'Of course, you poor darling, you were so brave for so long – I don't know how you bore it. But when you suddenly cracked, and told me all about it, I knew you had to have some help. I could see in your eyes that you'd never be able to fight out of this awful situation by your efforts.'

Your husband, Edna, has a fat neck full of wrinkles. His moustache is grey and looks rat-nibbled. He is kind and faithful. Mine is. . . .

She smelt the sharp, nostalgic freesia-scent again, and suddenly she was gulping back tears.

'Edna, I don't – '

'Darling. You're crying. Listen, I'm coming straight over to see you.'

'No, don't. *Don't*. I'll be all right. Please.'

'You don't *sound* all right.'

'Look, Edna, I'm going to ring off now and go and have a bath or something.'

'Good, darling, that's the best thing you could do. But you won't turn back, will you?'

'What do you mean,' Laura said hopelessly, 'turn back?'

'You won't talk yourself out of going ahead with the plan?'

Laura Daniel stared out of the window. The trees were gently nodding and waving, as if to invisible friends. Somewhere, her husband was walking down a street. Or sitting in a room. Or going up in a lift. Or lying in a bed? What horror waited to spring on her, tearing and trampling? What lay crouched among the summer leaves?

'Edna, I'll talk to you again. I'll just – '

'There's no need to talk to me again, darling. Just make that one appointment, to see Captain Grindle, and the whole thing – '

'*No!*'

The cry was torn from Laura's throat. It stabbed into the telephone, bounced back, and rolled harmlessly among the sofa cushions. She was defeated.

'Look, my love, you're overwrought. If you don't want me to come and see you, I won't, of course – '

'It's just that I – '

'But I really must help you. I tell you what. Are you doing anything tomorrow morning?'

'No. I – '

'Then what I'll do is this. I'll telephone the agency and tell them you can see Captain Grindle tomorrow morning, say about eleven. You'll only have to see him once, and have a very short talk with him. The rest can all be done through the post. There's no point in having it hanging over ... Laura, are you there?'

'Yes, I'm here.'

'Well, you go and have a nice bath and put on a pretty dress. I'm going to see you through this business, don't worry.'

'Edna, *please* don't do it. I don't want the man to come here. *Please*. If you do, I'll just ring them up and tell them it's a mistake and cancel the appointment.'

'Oh, no, you won't, darling. You're too unstrung to be able to do anything as decisive as that. I wouldn't be ringing them on your behalf if you were capable of dialling their number and speaking to them.'

'Edna, please – '

'Don't worry, darling. Ring off now. Everything'll be all right.'

The telephone rested.

Laura turned on the taps and got into the bath. The caress of warm water never failed to do something for her; for a moment her trouble seemed distant, irrelevant to the minute-to-minute business of living. Consciously taking advantage of this moment of liberation, she lay buoyed up and contained, planning a break-out from the prison of her misery. Surely there were ways of beating all this? The boys would help her. Two half-grown sons, their minds and bodies forming day by day. They needed her: Larry with his attractive, gawky diffidence, his fifteen-year-old colt's body, long-legged and beautiful in its awkwardness. She could live through him ... no, that was the wrong way to put it ... his life was his own, and so, God help her, was hers ... but he needed certain things which only a mother could give. He needed her more than calm, self-possessed Edward, who at thirteen had already taken on the manner and entered on the programme that were to be his for life. But even for Edward, there were things she could do. She could take an interest, advise, read up on anything he was interested in, become well-informed so that he could turn to her and feel respect for her usefulness. An adult person had so many ways and means of making inquiries into things ... *inquiries*! At the word's numbing impact, the lightness seemed to go out of her body, the water ceased to hold her, she lay on the floor of the bath like a dead beetle.

Never mind! Struggle on! She stood up, reached for her towel, and began to swish it vigorously across the skin of her back. Fight, Laura! Stand up and fight! You have the boys – a link with Bernard that none of those girls could ever have. She stepped out of the bath, and the movement brought her into view of her reflection in the mirror. Slack skin round the jaw. Two sons versus a firm, youthful skin. Two weekly letters from school versus an alabaster throat. Hockey-sticks and chemistry-sets versus a bed that Bernard looked forward to getting into.

Hounded by pain, she struggled into her clothes and almost ran along the landing to the boys' room. They had chosen to share one large room rather than two small ones, and they were equally insistent on having it left exactly as they arranged it, while they were away during term-time. She sank down, weeping, on Larry's bed. What could she offer, what could she do? How much longer could she postpone the time when they would read the unhappiness in her eyes?

If they were at home all the time it would be different. She longed, with a violence that surpassed her longing for her husband, for the thumping, cheerful, male-smelling physical presence of her sons. Cheerful? Yes, even through all their adolescent sulks and rebellions. It was optimistic misery, cheerful suffering, enmity and wrath that never doubted the possibility of a healed and restored future. They had time, like Edna, time to make mistakes and false starts, and still arrive at a happy sunlit point of rest.

Drying her tears, Laura went back to the bathroom and began slowly, methodically arranging her appearance. A cold courageous determination filled her veins and drove her heart forward in a steady rhythm, like an animal loping without fatigue. She would go where they went. If Larry and Edward, in their strange world of routines and alliances, could thrust like plants towards strength and maturity, so could she. As her body withered, her mind would be liberated, her eyes opened, her heart eased and consoled with love. Love? For the boys, primarily, but also for Bernard, in gratitude for his having given her the boys, in peaceful and generous recognition of all that they shared. A world enclosed, safe, utterly protected from the incursions of girls with soft, cascading hair and fragrant rounded limbs. Safe, safe, safe . . .

She was at the top of the stairs, about to come down, regal and unconquerable. Her new dress flattered her figure, her make-up was right, the letters from Larry and Edward were piled neatly in her writing desk, a solid testimony of her success as a human being. Nothing could shake her, she was a queen, vibrantly alive, commanding and forgiving. Then she heard the front door open, and Bernard's footstep as he went to hang up his hat and coat.

'Hello?' he called, on a rising, interrogative note. 'Laura? You at home?'

She stood, hidden by the curve of the staircase, and her heart changed from a loping animal to a pitiless hammer, crumbling her pride and her resolution.

'Any tea going?' Bernard's voice called, as his footsteps wandered towards the living-room.

What is her name?

Bernard, what have you been saying to her? Does she want you to leave me and marry her? But of course she does, doesn't she? Bernard, think of our sons! Why did you send them away to school, Larry and Edward, when I needed them so much?

In tears again, she went silently back into the boys' room. I want their clothes to wash, I want to lean over a tub and rinse out their sweaty shirts, I want to toil and bend my back like a poor woman, too tired to care what her husband does as long as he feeds the family and gives her money. Why did you take them away? Set them down among strangers who watch over their bodies and minds for money, in a town on the other side of England? You have your girl, Bernard, whoever she is (her

41

name? her colouring? does she make love impetuously or savour you slowly? why will my pain not kill me now, at once?).

Back to the bathroom, the astringent lotion, the cream, the make-up. Laura, you must fight and you must win. Down the stairs. If Bernard is clamouring for tea, that must surely mean he has not been at the girl's flat with her? Because surely she would have given him a cup of tea?

No. Home he comes for tea. Romance, excitement, sensuality, these do not coexist with steaming kettles and tea-leaves. At least let us hope so. Because if ever he finds all these things in one place, Laura . . .

She called, keeping her voice steady, 'Mrs Stevens has gone – I'll make some tea.' Into the kitchen. Get some practice at not crying – rehearse composure to the taps, the saucepans. What are the boys doing now? Who is making their tea? When will they have girls? Do they already lust after smooth necks, trim haunches, breasts well hidden under drip-dry fashion?

Going into the living-room with the tea-tray, she hated Bernard. Sitting in his armchair, leafing through a magazine, he smiled up at her with the old, programmed charm, and suddenly she saw him through Edna's eyes. A fifty-year-old lecher, sliding round corners, a dog licking a series of chop-bones.

'We're not doing anything tonight, are we?' he asked her casually, stirring his tea.

'No,' she answered. (When do we ever do anything? Have you ever noticed me for ten years? Even when we are side by side, putting on a social act?)

'Good,' he sighed, settling back in the chair. 'A nice little dinner à deux and then an hour or two's good music by courtesy of hi-fi. And so to bed. How's that for an evening?'

What's the matter, Bernard? Did she tire you out? Not so young as you were?

Something about her silence caught his attention, and he looked up. She stiffened. Oh, God, not the protective smile. Not the kindly-husband manner, the perfect marital butler drawing the corks.

'Something the matter, darling?'

'No,' she said, dropping the word like a dead bird into a well.

But he was getting out of his chair. Stop it, stop it, don't come near me or I'll smell her perfume. But she smelt nothing. He took her hands in his: cold and limp in warm and strong. Bernard, don't be unfair – I'm a woman too. Give me what you give her, or leave me alone.

'Tired? Was it a big day?'

'No. Tired with doing nothing, really. The fact is – I miss Larry and Edward.'

'They'll be home in three weeks.'

She shrugged. 'They're *never* home. The school-world encloses them even when they're here. Home just isn't real to them.'

He switched on the protective smile again. 'You're talking like a mum. Of course it's real. For a few years they talk about school, then for a few years they talk about university, but it's always home underneath it all. Home and you and me.'

And your girl? Invisibly with us? Present in the air we breathe? Laura fought to keep her hatred intact, but to her dismay it leaked out, lost its firmness, keeled over. He was so repulsively expert, Bernard, at keeping her in line, feeding her enough attention to stop her before she reached the point of madness, soothing her suffering before it drove her into a final wild insurrection. Kindness? It was no more than efficiency, the smooth working of his chosen scheme of life. If he kept her 'contented', she wouldn't bite, wouldn't interfere with his plans by plunging and rearing.

But it worked. Perhaps he really was kind ... just couldn't help it with the girls. Dinner for two? Any jobs needed? Should he prepare the vegetables? Mrs Stevens had left them all ready. Very well, he would lay the table, decant the wine, select the records for their evening's musical entertainment.

She watched him, in glances and short, intense stares, as they moved about the too-orderly house. It wasn't so much that he looked less than his age, she reflected, as that he made his age seem unimportant. Fifty, hair thinning, most of his teeth either crowned or false, but he made these things seem a joke. He moved his body with the casual grace of a man whose bones are soaked in pleasure. It's kept him young, she thought, stirring the white sauce and keeping the gas turned low. Do the girls think of him as old? A sugar-daddy? To Larry and Edward, what does he look like? A fogey? Father Christmas?

Bernard, unconscious of this flow of images, joked and chatted. He's being 'good company', she thought with a loud inner scream. We're good pals. Get on well together. God help me to find something like a human life. Let me be destitute under a hedge, trudging through the rain to a casual ward, let me be bed-ridden in a forgotten hospital, but let the content of my life be real and direct, not staged, not packaged by this smiling salesman of lies.

But by the time they sat facing each other, the thought had swung into place, 'At least he does smile.' Considering what a nuisance she must be to him at times, how much more difficult she made it for him to carry out his programme (arriving between every pair of sheets exactly on schedule), he treated her, after all, very amiably.

Still thinking this thought, turning it round in the luminous tank of her mind and examining its every colour and refraction, she arrived at the end of the meal. Bernard gallantly stacked the dishes into neat piles and loaded them on the tray, but she prevented him from carrying them out into the kitchen. 'I need to go anyway. I want to check the refrigerator and see if we're stocked up for the week-end.' He nodded and turned his attention to the gramophone, leaving her a much-needed avenue of escape. Once at the sanctuary of the sink, she clutched the taps. Could she go through with this evening? Sitting opposite him, with music prying at her clenched feelings, loosening and opening them out, would she not burst into tears and tell him about Captain Grindle?

Of course not. Captain Grindle was not here. He was in his own ugly home in the outer suburbs, a cheap tiled roof among tiled roofs, with a pot of ferns in the front window and a china dog barking soundlessly from the cabinet. Until tomorrow, he had no permission to exist.

When she returned to the living-room, Bernard had already clicked four long-playing records into place above the turntable. Considerately, he waited for Laura to settle into her chair by the fire before setting the machine in motion. Then there was a flat, pancake thud as the first record fell into place, followed by a short acid hiss and then the first notes of a symphony.

Sitting back, cradled by firelight and music, Laura searched her mind for any thought that would protect her against Captain Grindle. But all the time, as she sat there, the destroyer of this contentment was preparing his armoury. Who was Captain Grindle? Where had he been, what had he been doing, all the years till now? She saw him moving purposefully through the years: when she was a girl at school, he was already in the army, slowly and unswervingly ascending rank by rank; when Bernard first captivated her, gathered her up like an armful of lilies, carried her away to marriage and the sharp, unearthly intoxication of her suffering, Grindle had been eating plain and sustaining food (she saw his jaws working, heard the squeak of his knife on the plate), dressing and undressing, moving towards her like a whale through the sea of time. And now he was almost on her. Treacherous, helpful Edna had signalled her position, escape was impossible, and her destruction was certain, because it was not only Edna's will but her own pain that drove her on. Captain Grindle would enable her to know. And once she knew, she would have no choice but to lay her knowledge before Bernard. The result? – a show-down (as Edna would call it), a display of emotion, a shock, possibly a rush of warmth and a momentary happiness. And then, inevitably, the confrontation of stone wall by stone wall: a fading of sunlight: the accelerating end. The next time, or the next time but one, or the time after that, when Bernard felt himself attracted to a young, pretty woman, he would leave her, even if it meant abandoning a part of himself. Grindle was coming. The sharp, many-sided pain in her breast would not let her turn him away. His large, plain feet, in efficiently cleaned and neatly repaired shoes, would crunch tomorrow up the gravel path towards the front-door bell that would signal the end of her life. You can safely leave it to me, Mrs Daniel. The results of our investigations in a plain envelope. Ample evidence for divorce proceedings.

The records clashed and spun to their conclusion. Bernard Daniel's cigar ended its life as a merrily fuming butt in the grate. It was bed-time. As Laura undressed, folded her clothes, washed and prepared for the sleep that she knew would not come, she had a curiously strong sensation of being watched by two distinct pairs of eyes. Edna's eyes, hard, inquisitive and unsatisfied, took in every movement of her ageing body: behind her was the seamed, moustached face of Captain Grindle, peering conscientiously and preparing to write a report on what he was seeing.

Bernard sank into bed and lay drowsily waiting for her. For an instant Laura felt that she would throw herself down beside him in the luxury of tears. But she stiffened back into her false calm. How could she beg him to save her from Captain Grindle, when somewhere a girl lay resting, renewing herself for Bernard, between sheets still crumpled from her last encounter with him?

Laura Daniel sighed once, then got into bed, turned out the light and lay down. She heard her husband's breathing and felt the warm bulk of his body. But these things seemed remote and intangible, as if experienced by someone else. Turning on her side, she stared with wide motionless eyes at her approaching loneliness.

A Visit at Tea-Time

Williams had to turn back half-way down the drive. His mouth was dry and his heart had begun that old nervous pounding he thought he had outgrown. He went out through the gate again and stood by the hedge, out of sight of the house. If anyone happened to be watching through a window, he did not want to be seen behaving in an eccentric way.

'It's perfectly reasonable,' he said out loud, looking half-defiantly along the deserted pavement, its gutters full of fallen leaves. Thinking aloud was an old habit of his, but in this case he comforted himself with the thought that it was only natural to try out his voice before ringing the bell. It sounded rather dry and hoarse, but not impossibly so. 'It's quite reasonable,' he repeated. 'Why shouldn't I want to see it? I shan't be putting them to much trouble. And after fifteen years . . . !'

It occurred to him that, even standing in the shelter of the hedge, he was still visible from the attic window. How many autumn afternoons, exactly like this one, had he spent behind that window, intent on some dream-game which had gradually absorbed the entire landscape: the quiet, dignified houses, the trees, the railway bridge in the distance, the occasional passer-by or lonely sniffing dog. 'Why do you spend so much time in the attic?' he could hear his mother saying. She felt it was ungrateful of him, after they had given up one of the downstairs rooms and fitted it up as his play-room, that he played there so little, preferring the high, secret attic, so much more dream-provoking. The play-room was a challenge to activity with its electric railway system, its boxes of toys and puzzles, its busy clutter and the determinedly bright pictures on its walls. Only in the attic had he felt free to imagine his own world and live in it for hours at a time.

Fifteen years – surely that gave him the right to go up to the front door, ring the bell and make a simple request? Setting his shoulders back, he turned briskly into the drive and walked, without faltering, the whole way up to the front door. Some thirty yards, he estimated it now with his adult eye. The front garden did not seem to have changed much from what he remembered. It had been mainly grass and shrubs, and it was so still. But the gravel beneath his feet had a sharper crunch. It had either been recently renewed or was very well cared for: perhaps both.

When he pressed the bell he heard nothing. For a moment his nervousness threatened to come flooding back, at the thought that the bell might be out of order, which would present him with the choice of either using the knocker, an assertiveness he shrank from, or standing there until someone discovered him by accident. But he pulled himself together before his control began to slip. It was a big house, and the bell rang in a distant room, probably with at least two shut doors between it and the front entrance. He had a sudden mental picture of the interior of the house, and in particular of the kitchen: warm and bright, with a fly-paper hanging from the ceiling and Frances setting out the tea-things. He would just have come in from school, his satchel and blue macintosh would be carelessly looped behind the door, and Frances would be getting tea and bread-and-butter just for the two of them, to fill the gap till seven o'clock. Of course it was only in later years that he had been allowed to have dinner with his parents at seven o'clock, after he was ten . . . or would it be eleven?

He heard Frances coming to the door. Her slow footsteps. Of course it could not really be Frances, she was dead and he had been to her funeral. But he could see her so plainly, and it was so impossible to imagine the kitchen without Frances, especially on an autumn afternoon with the light beginning to fade and the tea-things on the table, as they must surely be . . . Frances! Why did we have to leave this house, why did you have to die, why did it all have to come to an end?

The hallucination vanished in an instant. Even as the door began to open, before he could even glimpse the figure he was about to see, he knew it would not be Frances. All the same, he was nonplussed.

Pale blue eyes that looked curiously flat, as if they were painted on a sheet of paper rather than set in a human face. Long, narrow features, iron-grey bun, cool grey nylon overall. Was she the housekeeper? Or . . . ?

'Good afternoon. I wonder if I might speak to . . .' Oh, for the days before he was born, when the door was opened by a servant in a mob-cap (whatever that was) and one simply said, 'Is the master in?'!

The woman stood, waiting, holding the door-knob in her hand.

'Is the – occupier – er, the master of the house at home?' Williams asked.

'The master of the house?' the woman echoed. Her voice, flat and without modulations, made the phrase sound alien, ridiculous and yet sinister.

Williams forced himself to be bright. 'You see, it's like this,' he said, creasing his face into an ironic, self-deprecating smile, conveying that he knew how absurd he was but nevertheless forgave himself for it out of a large and humane tolerance, a fully civilized man among his peers, 'I don't actually know who lives here, but – '

'You don't know who lives here?' the woman echoed again. Once more his own words, held up flatly for his inspection, seemed futile and yet full of menace.

'It's quite simple, actually,' he said, beginning again with a good-humoured patience that inwardly surprised him. 'This house – '

'We don't want to buy anything,' the woman suddenly interposed. With rising panic he saw that she was beginning to close the door against him. *Frances, Frances, where are you?*

'I'm not selling anything.' He began to talk quickly. 'I simply wanted to ask a very small favour of whoever happens to live here now. You see, I was born in this house.'

'D'you want to see Mr Edmundson?' the housekeeper – for it must be she – chose this moment to ask.

Williams nodded dumbly. He wanted to be done with this woman, whose function in life was so obviously to refuse, to deny, to guard the house against intruders. If she knew the request he had come to make, she would be quite likely to refuse it from sheer force of habit. Whereas the owner of the house, this Edmundson, could never be so insanely grudging as to. . . . She was motioning him to enter, to follow her through the hall and into the drawing-room. That was what they had always called this room, rather small and sunless by comparison with the others on the ground floor. It was clear that the Edmundsons used it, just as his own parents had done, as a dumping-ground for unexpected visitors, where they could be out of the way until the right member of the family could attend to them. *Nothing has changed*, he felt suddenly. The house was lived in, warmed, lighted, its arteries aglow with the essence that made it a living thing, able to welcome him – to extend its own welcome, if need be, over the heads of the present inhabitants.

The room, however, had changed almost out of recognition. The furniture was modern, with that dead, unreverberating modernity that seems to belong to the laboratory and the machine-shop, never to humanity. As if to compensate for the inert silence of the rubber-upholstered armchairs, the blankness of the sensible sofa, the impersonal grin of the electric fire, the wallpaper and curtains carried busy little patterns which did their best to call out in high, childish voices, though anything in the nature of communication remained obstinately out of their reach.

Income? Tastes? Williams pondered. A husband who worked for a news agency? A wife who had been to art school? *Something* must have caused this bright, dead overlay of up-to-date-ness, this combination of bright colours which only succeeded in conveying a hopeless inner drabness. He moved to the window. The electric light in the room made the garden seem dusky, but there was plenty of daylight still, and he ought to be able to –

'Sorry to keep you waiting,' said a voice behind him. 'You wanted to see me about something?'

Edmundson. Fat, frog-like: glasses: prosperous business exterior: accent originally demotic: not altogether sure of himself, but (therefore?) outwardly confident and assertive.

'My name is Williams.' He retreated from the frog-eyes into a grave, almost eighteenth-century formality. 'I hate to disturb you, but I have a very small request which I hope you will grant.'

'Let me know what it is,' said Edmundson, matter-of-fact and alert.

'That won't take long. I was born here. We lived here till I was fifteen. Then my father died and we moved to a place in Kent to be near some relatives of my mother's. I've never been back since – not even to the town, still less to this house. I'm thirty now, so that makes fifteen years.'

Edmundson waited. His expression said, 'Well?'

'My father planted a tree in the garden when I was born. He said he wanted the two forms of life to grow up together, though of course it would outlive me. It was a beech.'

'Well?' Edmundson said it with his voice this time.

'I just wanted to look at the tree. See how big it had grown.'

'A very natural wish,' said Edmundson.

'I could just slip into the garden and look at it, and then make my way round the side of the house. I needn't disturb you again. It's good of you to – '

'It doesn't exist any more,' Edmundson interrupted, flatly.

'It doesn't . . . ?'

'I had it cut down. It was in an awkward position. It shaded a large part of the lawn and it didn't really compensate by breaking the wind much.'

'You . . .'

'The prevailing winds here, as you'll remember, are mostly south-west. The tree hardly gave any shelter. All it did was to block the sunlight from that bit of the lawn. So my wife and I agreed, after trying it for one summer, that we'd be better off without it.'

On the words 'my wife' Mrs Edmundson entered, for all the world as if she had listened through the keyhole for her cue. Yet one look at her revealed a person who could never have listened at keyholes. Frank, open, modern, all air and light and sensibleness, with no nonsense and no dark corners beyond the reach of consciousness. Younger than her husband, and conscious of her youth as something to be lived up to: he must be rising fifty, she barely thirty, and she evidently saw it as a duty (the furniture! the curtains!) to represent her generation.

'This is my wife: Mr Williams:' Edmundson introduced them the wrong way round, the woman to the man, though whether this was out of some vestigial *gaucherie* or from an impulse of genuine courtesy, to set protocol aside and give precedence to the visitor, Williams did not know and would never know. 'I'm afraid poor Mr Williams has had a journey for nothing,' he went on, trying to ride over the situation with polite, heavy geniality. 'He was born in this house, and the beech tree we cut down – you remember? – was planted to commemorate his birth.'

Williams shifted uneasily from one foot to the other, irritated by the pompous phrasing. 'To commemorate his birth' made him sound like a dead, bald-headed politician. 'Hardly that,' he said. 'To share my life.'

'Well, it shared a quarter of a century of your life,' Edmundson put in, his matter-of-fact voice reaching towards a cadence of consolation. 'It must have been at least twenty-five years old when we – removed it.' He didn't like to say 'we cut it down'; oaf as he was, the symbolism was too harsh for him.

It was the wife, brisk, poodle-haired, secure in a bright woollen dress, who now moved in to take charge of the situation. 'I don't quite understand,' though she obviously understood perfectly. 'D'you mean Mr Williams wanted to see how his tree was getting on?' Her phrasing was intended to show, and did show, a Nanny-bright disapproval of childish whims.

'In a way, yes,' said Williams, trying to keep his voice level. He hated her, was sure she had been behind the murder of his tree, with her rational machine-turned little mind.

'What a pity,' she said, drawing a light breath. 'Well, it looks as if that particular quest is over, doesn't it? You'll have to go through the rest of your life without your *Doppelgänger*.'

'You don't have to make fun of me,' said Williams calmly.

'I'm not. I'm simply saying that from now on you'll have to adjust to the knowledge that you're on your own.'

Suddenly Williams understood. *Psychology.*

'You mean it's infantile regression for me to want to see my tree?'

'Not strictly speaking. Infantile regression comes out in other ways. But it *is* clinging to the past, isn't it?'

'It's only the past because you've cut it down. If it were alive, growing out there, it would be the present.'

'Nonsense. If it was the present you were interested in, any tree would do. You've made a symbol out of that particular tree because your father planted it. You should go and get your father to plant another.'

'He's dead,' said Williams. 'He died in this house and after he was dead we couldn't afford to live here any more.'

'But there was a piece of your life left growing here and that's what you came back to see.'

'Correct.'

'But surely you can see that you can't live like that? I mean, I'm sorry your tree isn't here, but isn't it a good thing for you, in a way? To know that you've got to carry on with your life independently, not leaning on outside circumstances?'

'I suppose,' Williams said carefully, to keep himself from striking her, 'by "outside circumstances" you mean things like the memory of my father?'

'I mean,' she gestured impatiently, 'all the clutter and the junk that one's apt to cling to instead of just living one's life in a straight line.'

Edmundson, a busy man, intervened. 'Well, I hardly think there's any point in discussing it in those terms. The plain fact is that the garden became ours when we acquired the house, and it was our own decision which trees to leave and which to cut down.' This time he had *said* it, perhaps gaining confidence from his wife's textbook prattle. 'I hardly think we need keep Mr Williams any longer, unless he would like a cup of tea before going.'

Instead of answering, Williams stared at Mrs Edmundson. Her skin was bad, he noticed – full of open pores and already, at her age, rather loose-fitting. He wondered what enjoyment she got with her husband. Surely her eyes would be brighter, if he was any use to her. And she would live through her body and not through her psychology lecture-notes. But if that were so, of course, she would have understood that living things matter, that they are not simply objects that give shelter or don't give shelter.

What was the use? 'Thank you for the offer of tea,' he said, addressing husband and wife impartially, though he noticed she had said nothing. 'But I'd better be getting off to the station. I'm sorry I troubled you for nothing.'

Edmundson produced a smile, doubtless largely of relief at bringing the interview to a peaceable end. His wife, her eyelids snapping angrily, was evidently disappointed that Williams had not troubled to quarrel with her.

'I expect you're very cross with us,' she said, meaning that she hoped he was, 'but perhaps when you think it over afterwards you'll find that we did you a favour.'

'A favour?' Williams murmured, perfunctorily ironic: in his eyes she already belonged to the past, that category she herself had declared worthless.

'Liberated you from your father. Try to look at it that way.'

He half-bowed, gravely indifferent, and said soothingly, 'I'll see myself out.' It would depress him too much to encounter again the nylon-clad housekeeper. After fifteen years, his tone reminded them, he should know his way to the front door.

He reached it unmolested, turned the Yale knob and went out. By comparison with the deadness inside the house, the garden seemed boisterous with life: a light breeze had sprung up, boughs danced lightly and shrubs, their shapes magnified in the dusk, seemed like hirsute animals standing still to be stroked and fed.

The front door safely shut behind him, the Edmundsons and their housekeeper already receding into history, Williams stood and looked around. They had spoilt the house for him, they had chased away the ghost of Frances and with it his own small ghost – but the garden, vivid among its stirring shadows, wore a secret, invulnerable air. The soil into which his fingers had plunged so many thousands of times, the grass and stones which had been so vividly before his eyes, in the days when he carried his head only three or four feet above them – no Edmundson could take them away; they belonged to him as surely as the cells of his own body.,

The path led round the house, to the back garden. Why not – just one look? His feet moved of their own accord, following the right-angled crazy paving towards their own past. The breeze puffed lightly at his bare head. Elation swelled in his veins.

The back garden was larger than he remembered it. Perhaps in those days, when it was his much-trodden kingdom, he had scaled it down to his own size. Now, pleasantly unkempt (evidently the Edmundsons preferred an indoor life) it seemed to his dusk-sharpened eyes to ramble like a prairie.

Where had the tree stood? He owed it, at least, that final salute – to locate the patch of air which, if it were still living, its branches would proudly enclose in a basket of leaf and bark. Besides, he was curious. He wanted to know whether, in her insane spite against his tree (for she must have known, intuitively, that it belonged to his world and rejected hers), the woman had given orders that the very roots be dragged from the earth. Or would he find a tidily sawn-off stump, something to touch with his hand in a final, casual blessing?

Over *there*, it had been: more or less in that corner of the lawn . . . he began to move towards the spot his eye had selected. And he had taken perhaps three steps before the small, high voice called 'Stop! Or they'll see you!'

Halting, he looked round. 'Where are you?' he said into the windy shadows.

'Here. In the tree. D'you want me to come down? D'you need help?'

'Yes,' Williams said. 'I need help.'

There was a rustling scrape of leather on bark, and the boy stood at his side. Seven? Eight? Grave-faced, in forty years he would probably look like his father, but this evening he was still secure within his own appearance.

'They'll see you,' the child whispered, 'if you don't stand quite still. They have their observation post *there*,' he pointed, 'on top of the shed?

Williams, armoured in grown-up dullness, had assumed at first that 'they' referred to the boy's parents. But an observation post on top of the shed?

'Who are they?' he asked in an urgent, hushed voice.

'The Eskimos,' the boy replied, staring ahead of him.

'And if I stand quite still?'

'They won't see you. You'll sort of merge into the tree-trunks.'

The lawn was quite bare. Now that Williams' birth-tree had

gone, the only tree of any size was some yards away, the one the child had scrambled down.

'Yes,' said Williams. 'I can imagine that Eskimos would have trouble spotting people among tree-trunks. They'd have no practice.'

'It's all new to them,' the boy explained. 'They've never seen trees before. And this is a dense forest. You can't go straight through it. You have to move like this.' He began to weave forward, gliding round the rotundity of the trunks.

'What kind of weapons have the Eskimos?' Williams asked.

'Crossbows. They shoot flint-headed arrows. If one were to hit you, you'd be split straight in half.'

'Crossbows, eh?' said Williams, peering through the trees. 'And what do they use at close quarters?'

'At what?'

'When they fight hand to hand?'

The boy shook his head. 'They never do that. They die if they leave the snow and ice. They can't enter the forest. All they can do is to stay in the cold part, with snow and ice. That comes up to the edge of the lawn. The lawn's all dense forest.'

Crouching beside the tense little figure, peering towards the Eskimos with their crossbows, Williams felt his frame gripped by a healing shudder of pure gratitude. *The lawn is dense forest,* he sang to himself. *All they can do is stay in the cold part.*

'Who sent the Eskimos here?' he asked.

'Nobody sent them,' said the child indifferently. 'They just come because they want to leave the snow and ice. But the forest stops them. All they can do is let off their flint arrows. In the morning, when I first come out, the forest's full of them. They fire them all night. I hear them when I lie in bed. But it doesn't matter – they never hit the birds. And they can't do the trees any harm because the trees have a special hard bark.'

'What do you do with the flint arrows? Do you pick them up?'

'I collect them. I'm building a fortress with a flint wall. That was what I was doing in the tree – noting the places where the arrows fell. They're very useful to me.'

A thin, house-proud voice called, 'David! Tea!'

'That's Mrs Eggleton. She gives me my breakfast and my tea. I have lunch with Mummy and Daddy, though. I have to go in now. Be careful of the Eskimos if you stay.'

'I'll make a noise like a walrus,' said Williams. 'Then perhaps they'll throw some harpoons. You'll be able to pick them up. They're ivory. You can make all sorts of things out of them.'

'Don't let them hit you,' David warned. 'They're very good aimers.'

'Ah, but I'm a good dodger. I'll be safely behind a tree-trunk.'

'All right. I'll look for the harpoons in the morning. Thanks,' he called over his shoulder, running towards the repeated querulous crying of his name.

'The lawn is a dense forest,' Williams said to himself. He sniggered, then laughed freely. The Eskimos glared at him from the dark corner behind the shed. 'Shoot, shoot!' he called to them. 'I'm a walrus!' Uncertain what kind of sound a walrus should make, he trumpeted, then skipped behind an armoured tree-trunk as the harpoons flashed through the air. One, two, three gleaming harpoons of ivory, for David to find in the morning.

Trumpeting, he skipped from tree to tree, hoping to draw their fire, but they had become more careful. Peering cautiously round a trunk near the edge of the lawn, he became aware, suddenly, of a neat platter of wood, shaved off at ground level. His tree! From its thickness he could make a rapid calculation of its height, and the reach of its branches.

'Hello,' he said to it, looking straight into the thickest part of its foliage. 'I'm back. I still exist. But it isn't I who matter – it's David. Help him, won't you? Let him win his battle against the Eskimos?'

For a moment he saw himself, chillingly, through the eyes of Mrs Edmundson. Talking, *out loud*, to a tree that wasn't even there! At the thought of her taut, disapproving face, Williams burst out laughing. 'Eskimos,' he said through his puffing explosions of mirth. Stepping warily, circling the tree trunks, Williams walked back across the lawn. It seemed to him, as he went up the path for the last time, and turned to look once more at the garden, that the darkening air was alive with the rustle of branches.

Manhood

Swiftly free-wheeling, their breath coming easily, the man and the boy steered their bicycles down the short dip which led them from woodland into open country. Then they looked ahead and saw that the road began to climb.

'Now, Rob,' said Mr Willison, settling his plump haunches firmly on the saddle, 'just up that rise and we'll get off and have a good rest.'

'Can't we rest now?' the boy asked. 'My legs feel all funny. As if they're turning to water.'

'Rest at the top,' said Mr Willison firmly. 'Remember what I told you? The first thing any athlete has to learn is to break the fatigue barrier.'

'I've broken it already. I was feeling tired when we were going along the main road and I – '

'When fatigue sets in, the thing to do is to keep going until it wears off. Then you get your second wind and your second endurance.'

'I've already done that.'

'Up we go,' said Mr Willison, 'and at the top we'll have a good rest.' He panted slightly and stood on his pedals, causing his machine to sway from side to side in a laboured manner. Rob, falling silent, pushed doggedly at his pedals. Slowly, the pair wavered up the straight road to the top. Once there, Mr Willison dismounted with exaggerated steadiness, laid his bicycle carefully on its side, and spread his jacket on the ground before sinking down to rest. Rob slid hastily from the saddle and flung himself full-length on the grass.

'Don't lie there,' said his father. 'You'll catch cold.'

'I'm all right. I'm warm.'

'Come and sit on this. When you're over-heated, that's just when you're prone to – '

'I'm all *right*, Dad. I want to lie here. My back aches.'

'Your back needs strengthening, that's why it aches. It's a pity we don't live near a river where you could get some rowing.'

The boy did not answer, and Mr Willison, aware that he was beginning to sound like a nagging, over-anxious parent, allowed himself to be defeated and did not press the suggestion about Rob's coming to sit on his jacket. Instead, he waited a moment and then glanced at his watch.

'Twenty to twelve. We must get going in a minute.'

'*What*? I thought we were going to have a rest.'

'Well, we're having one, aren't we?' said Mr Willison reasonably. 'I've got my breath back, so surely you must have.'

'My back still aches. I want to lie here a bit.'

'Sorry,' said Mr Willison, getting up and moving over to his bicycle. 'We've got at least twelve miles to do and lunch is at one.'

'Dad, why did we have to come so far if we've got to get back for one o'clock? I know, let's find a telephone box and ring up Mum and tell her we – '

'Nothing doing. There's no reason why two fit men shouldn't cycle twelve miles in an hour and ten minutes.'

'But we've already done about a million miles.'

'We've done about fourteen, by my estimation,' said Mr Willison stiffly. 'What's the good of going for a bike ride if you don't cover a bit of distance?'

He picked up his bicycle and stood waiting. Rob, with his hand over his eyes, lay motionless on the grass. His legs looked thin and white among the rich grass.

'Come on, Rob.'

The boy showed no sign of having heard. Mr Willison got on to his bicycle and began to ride slowly away. 'Rob,' he called over his shoulder, 'I'm going.'

Rob lay like a sullen corpse by the roadside. He looked horribly like the victim of an accident, unmarked but dead from internal injuries. Mr Willison cycled fifty yards, then a hundred, then turned in a short, irritable circle and came back to where his son lay.

'Rob, is there something the matter or are you just being awkward?'

The boy removed his hand and looked up into his father's face. His eyes were surprisingly mild: there was no fire of rebellion in them.

'I'm tired and my back aches. I can't go on yet.'

'Look, Rob,' said Mr Willison gently, 'I wasn't going to tell you this, because I meant it to be a surprise, but when you get home you'll find a present waiting for you.'

'What kind of present?'

'Something very special I've bought for you. The man's coming this morning to fix it up. That's one reason why I suggested a bike ride this morning. He'll have done it by now.'

'What is it?'

'Aha. It's a surprise. Come on, get on your bike and let's go home and see.'

Rob sat up, then slowly clambered to his feet. 'Isn't there a short cut home?'

'I'm afraid not. It's only twelve miles.'

Rob said nothing.

'And a lot of that's downhill,' Mr Willison added brightly. His own legs were tired and his muscles fluttered unpleasantly. In addition, he suddenly realized he was very thirsty. Rob, still without speaking, picked up his bicycle, and they pedalled away.

'Where is he?' Mrs Willison asked, coming into the garage.

'Gone up to his room,' said Mr Willison. He doubled his fist and gave the punch-ball a thudding blow. 'Seems to have fixed it pretty firmly. You gave him the instructions, I suppose.'

'What's he doing up in his room? It's lunch-time.'

'He said he wanted to rest a bit.'

'I hope you're satisfied,' said Mrs Willison. 'A lad of thirteen, nearly fourteen years of age, just when he should have a really big appetite, and when the lunch is put on the table he's *resting* – '

'Now look, I know what I'm – '

'Lying down in his room, resting, too tired to eat because you've dragged him up hill and down dale on one of your – '

'We did nothing that couldn't be reasonably expected of a boy of his age.'

'How do you know?' Mrs Willison demanded. 'You never did anything of that kind when you were a boy. How do you know what can be reasonably –'

'Now look,' said Mr Willison again. 'When I was a boy, it was study, study, study all the time, with the fear of unemployment and insecurity in everybody's mind. I was never even given a bicycle. I never boxed, I never rowed, I never did anything to develop my physique. It was just work, work, work; pass this exam, get that certificate. Well, I did it and now I'm qualified and in a secure job. But you know as well as I do that they let me down. Nobody encouraged me to build myself up.'

'Well, what does it matter? You're all right –'

'Grace!' Mr Willison interrupted sharply. 'I am not all right and you know it. I am under average height, my chest is flat and I'm –'

'What nonsense. You're taller than I am and I'm –'

'No son of mine is going to grow up with the same wretched physical heritage that I –'

'No, he'll just have heart disease through overtaxing his strength, because you haven't got the common sense to –'

'His heart is one hundred per cent all right. Not three weeks have gone by since the doctor looked at him.'

'Well, why does he get so over-tired if he's all right? Why is he lying down now instead of coming to the table, a boy of his age?'

A slender shadow blocked part of the dazzling sun in the doorway. Looking up simultaneously, the Willisons greeted their son.

'Lunch ready, Mum? I'm hungry.'

'Ready when you are,' Grace Willison beamed. 'Just wash your hands and come to the table.'

'Look, Rob,' said Mr Willison. 'If you hit it with your left hand and then catch it on the rebound with your right, it's excellent ring training.' He dealt the punch-ball two amateurish blows. 'That's what they call a right cross,' he said.

'I think it's fine. I'll have some fun with it,' said Rob. He watched mildly as his father peeled off the padded mittens.

'Here, slip these on,' said Mr Willison. 'They're just training gloves. They harden your fists. Of course, we can get a pair of proper gloves later. But these are specially for use with the ball.'

'Lunch,' called Mrs Willison from the house.

'Take a punch at it,' Mr Willison urged.

'Let's go and eat.'

'Go on. One punch before you go in. I haven't seen you hit it yet.'

Rob took the gloves, put on the right-hand one, and gave the punch-ball one conscientious blow, aiming at the exact centre. 'Now let's go in,' he said.

'Lunch!'

'All right. We're coming . . .'

'Five feet eight, Rob,' said Mr Willison, folding up the wooden ruler. 'You're taller than I am. This is a great landmark.'

'Only *just* taller.'

'But you're growing all the time. Now all you have to do is to start growing outwards as well as upwards. We'll have you in the middle of that scrum. The heaviest forward in the pack.'

Rob picked up his shirt and began uncertainly poking his arms into the sleeves.

'When do they pick the team?' Mr Willison asked. 'I should have thought they'd have done it by now.'

'They have done it,' said Rob. He bent down to pick up his socks from under a chair.

'They have? And you –'

'I wasn't selected,' said the boy, looking intently at the socks as if trying to detect minute differences in colour and weave.

Mr Willison opened his mouth, closed it again, and stood for a moment looking out of the window. Then he gently laid his hand on his son's shoulder. 'Bad luck,' he said quietly.

'I tried hard,' said Rob quickly.

'I'm sure you did.'

'I played my hardest in the trial games.'

'It's just bad luck,' said Mr Willison. 'It could happen to anybody.'

There was silence as they both continued with their dressing.

A faint smell of frying rose into the air, and they could hear Mrs Willison laying the table for breakfast.

'That's it, then, for this season,' said Mr Willison, as if to himself.

'I forgot to tell you, though,' said Rob. 'I was selected for the boxing team.'

'You *were*? I didn't know the school had one.'

'It's new. Just formed. They had some trials for it at the end of last term. I found my punching was better than most people's because I'd been getting plenty of practice with the ball.'

Mr Willison put out a hand and felt Rob's biceps. 'Not bad, not bad at all,' he said critically. 'But if you're going to be a boxer and represent the school, you'll need more power up there. I tell you what. We'll train together.'

'That'll be fun,' said Rob. 'I'm training at school too.'

'What weight do they put you in?'

'It isn't weight, it's age. Under fifteen. Then when you get over fifteen you get classified into weights.'

'Well,' said Mr Willison, tying his tie, 'you'll be in a good position for the under-fifteens. You've got six months to play with. And there's no reason why you shouldn't steadily put muscle on all the time. I suppose you'll be entered as a team, for tournaments and things?'

'Yes. There's a big one at the end of next term. I'll be in that.'

Confident, joking, they went down to breakfast. 'Two eggs for Rob, Mum,' said Mr Willison. 'He's in training. He's going to be a heavyweight.'

'A heavyweight what?' Mrs Willison asked, teapot in hand.

'Boxer,' Rob smiled.

Grace Willison put down the teapot, her lips compressed, and looked from one to the other. '*Boxing*?' she repeated.

'Boxing,' Mr Willison replied calmly.

'Over my dead body,' said Mrs Willison. 'That's one sport I'm definite that he's never going in for.'

'Too late. They've picked him for the under-fifteens. He's had trials and everything.

'Is this true, Rob?' she demanded.

'Yes,' said the boy, eating rapidly.

'Well, you can just tell them you're dropping it. Baroness Summerskill – '

'To hell with Baroness Summerskill!' her husband shouted. 'The first time he gets a chance to do something, the first time he gets picked for a team and given a chance to show what he's made of, and you have to bring up Baroness Summerskill.'

'But it injures their brains! All those blows on the front of the skull. I've read about it – '

'Injures their brains!' Mr Willison snorted. 'Has it injured Ingemar Johansson's brain? Why, he's one of the acutest business men in the world!'

'Rob,' said Mrs Willison steadily, 'when you get to school, go and see the sports master and tell him you're giving up boxing.'

'There isn't a sports master. All the masters do bits of it at different times.'

'There must be one who's in charge of the boxing. All you have to do is tell him – '

'Are you ready, Rob?' said Mr Willison. 'You'll be late for school if you don't go.'

'I'm in plenty of time, Dad. I haven't finished my breakfast.'

'Never mind, push along, old son. You've had your egg and bacon, that's what matters. I want to talk to your mother.'

Cramming a piece of dry toast into his mouth, the boy picked up his satchel and wandered from the room. Husband and wife sat back, glaring hot-eyed at each other.

The quarrel began, and continued for many days. In the end it was decided that Rob should continue boxing until he had represented the school at the tournament in March of the following year, and should then give it up.

'Ninety-six, ninety-seven, nighty-eight, ninety-nine, a hundred,' Mr Willison counted. 'Right, that's it. Now go and take your shower and get into bed.'

'I don't feel tired, honestly,' Rob protested.

'Who's manager here, you or me?' Mr Willison asked bluffly. 'I'm in charge of training and you can't say my methods don't work. Fifteen solid weeks and you start questioning my decisions on the very night of the fight?'

'It just seems silly to go to bed when I'm not –'

'My dear Rob, please trust me. No boxer ever went into a big fight without spending an hour or two in bed, resting, just before going to his dressing-room.'

'All right. But I bet none of the others are bothering to do all this.'

'That's exactly why you're going to be better than the others. Now go and get your shower before you catch cold. Leave the skipping-rope, I'll put it away.'

After Rob had gone, Mr Willison folded the skipping-rope into a neat ball and packed it away in the case that contained the boy's gloves, silk dressing gown, lace-up boxing boots, and trunks with the school badge sewn into the correct position on the right leg. There would be no harm in a little skipping, to limber up and conquer his nervousness while waiting to go on. Humming, he snapped down the catches of the small leather case and went into the house.

Mrs Willison did not lift her eyes from the television set as he entered. 'All ready now, Mother,' said Mr Willison. 'He's going to rest in bed now, and go along at about six o'clock. I'll go with him and wait till the doors open to be sure of a ringside seat.' He sat down on the sofa beside his wife, and tried to put his arm round her. 'Come on, love,' he said coaxingly. 'Don't spoil my big night.'

She turned to him and he was startled to see her eyes brimming with angry tears. 'What about my big night?' she asked, her voice harsh. 'Fourteen years ago, remember? When he came into the world.'

'Well, what about it?' Mr Willison parried, uneasily aware that the television set was quacking and signalling on the fringe of his attention, turning the scene from clumsy tragedy into a clumsier farce.

'Why didn't you tell me then?' she sobbed. 'Why did you let me have a son if all you were interested in was having him punched to death by a lot of rough bullet-headed louts who –'

'Take a grip on yourself, Grace. A punch on the nose won't hurt him.'

'You're an unnatural father,' she keened. 'I don't know how you can bear to send him into that ring to be beaten and thumped – Oh, why can't you stop him now? Keep him at home? There's no *law* that compels us to – '

'That's where you're wrong, Grace,' said Mr Willison sternly. 'There is a law. The unalterable law of nature that says that the young males of the species indulge in manly trials of strength. Think of all the other lads who are going into the ring tonight. D'you think their mothers are sitting about crying and kicking up a fuss? No – they're proud to have strong, masculine sons who can stand up in the ring and take a few punches.'

'Go away, please,' said Mrs Willison, sinking back with closed eyes. 'Just go right away and don't come near me until it's all over.'

'Grace!'

'Please. Please leave me alone. I can't bear to look at you and I can't bear to hear you.'

'You're hysterical,' said Mr Willison bitterly. Rising, he went out into the hall and called up the stairs. 'Are you in bed, Rob?'

There was a slight pause and then Rob's voice called faintly, 'Could you come up, Dad?'

'Come up? Why? Is something the matter?'

'Could you come up?'

Mr Willison ran up the stairs. 'What is it?' he panted. 'D'you want something?'

'I think I've got appendicitis,' said Rob. He lay squinting among the pillows, his face suddenly narrow and crafty.

'I don't believe you,' said Mr Willison shortly. 'I've supervised your training for fifteen weeks and I know you're as fit as a fiddle. You can't possibly have anything wrong with you.'

'I've got a terrible pain in my side,' said Rob. 'Low down on the right-hand side. That's where appendicitis comes, isn't it?'

Mr Willison sat down on the bed. 'Listen, Rob,' he said. 'Don't do this to me. All I'm asking you to do is to go into the ring and have one bout. You've been picked for the school team and everyone's depending on you.'

'I'll die if you don't get the doctor,' Rob suddenly hissed. 'Mum!' he shouted.

Mrs Willison came bounding up the stairs. 'What is it, my pet?'

'My stomach hurts. Low down on the right-hand side.'

'Appendicitis!' She whirled to face Mr Willison. 'That's what comes of your foolishness!'

'I don't believe it,' said Mr Willison. He went out of the bedroom and down the stairs. The television was still jabbering in the living-room, and for fifteen minutes Mr Willison forced himself to sit staring at the strident puppets, glistening in metallic light, as they enacted their Lilliputian rituals. Then he went up to the bedroom again. Mrs Willison was bathing Rob's forehead.

'His temperature's normal,' she said.

'Of course his temperature's normal,' said Mr Willison. 'He doesn't want to fight, that's all.'

'Fetch the doctor,' said a voice from under the cold flannel that swathed Rob's face.

'We will, pet, if you don't get better very soon,' said Mrs Willison, darting a murderous glance at her husband.

Mr Willison slowly went downstairs. For a moment he stood looking at the telephone, then picked it up and dialled the number of the grammar school. No one answered. He replaced the receiver, went to the foot of the stairs and called, 'What's the name of the master in charge of this tournament?'

'I don't know,' Rob called weakly.

'You told me you'd been training with Mr Granger,' Mr Willison called. 'Would he know anything about it?'

Rob did not answer, so Mr Willison looked up all the Grangers in the telephone book. There were four in the town, but only one was M.A. 'That's him,' said Mr Willison. With lead in his heart and ice in his fingers, he dialled the number.

Mrs Granger fetched Mr Granger. Yes, he taught at the school. He was the right man. What could he do for Mr Willison?

'It's about tonight's boxing tournament.'

'Sorry, what? The line's bad.'

'*Tonight's boxing tournament.*'

'Have you got the right person?'

'You teach my son, Rob – we've just agreed on that. Well,

it's about the boxing tournament he's supposed to be taking part in tonight.'

'Where?'

'Where? At the school, of course. He's representing the under-fifteens.'

There was a pause. 'I'm not quite sure what mistake you're making, Mr Willison, but I think you've got hold of the wrong end of at least one stick.' A hearty, defensive laugh. 'If Rob belongs to a boxing-club it's certainly news to me, but in any case it can't be anything to do with the school. We don't go in for boxing.'

'Don't go in for it?'

'We don't offer it. It's not in our curriculum.'

'Oh,' said Mr Willison. 'Oh. Thank you. I must have – well, thank you.'

'Not at all. I'm glad to answer any queries. Everything's all right, I trust?'

'Oh, yes,' said Mr Willison, 'yes, thanks. Everything's all right.'

He put down the telephone, hesitated, then turned and began slowly to climb the stairs.

Darkness

'You'd better go,' they warned me.

'Already?' I asked.

'Jesus puts the lights out early,' they said, 'he wants to get back home to his wife.'

And they all laughed. They were the kind of nice, silly young foreigners, Americans and English, who find never-failing humour in the fact that Spaniards use 'Jesus' as a name for ordinary people and not just for Jesus Christ.

Jesus was the man in charge of the power supply. He was supposed to keep it going till twelve o'clock at night, but he was a young man who had recently married a still younger wife, and nobody in the village blamed him for that chronically fast watch of his, which generally showed midnight twenty minutes ahead of time. Especially since he had to get back to the controls at five in the morning. The villagers got up early and went to bed early. No doubt Jesus would have been able to turn the electricity off and go home at ten every night if it had not been for people like us: tourists, holidaymakers, refugees from our own bleak northern cities where the powerful arc lamps and coloured neon signs glared down all night long on the rain-soaked pavements.

Thinking of Jesus and how he must hate my friends and me, I got up, thanked my hosts, and moved to the door. I needed the street lamps. Their house stood on the tip of the sharp little hill that crowned the village, and I did not want to climb down the steep cobbled steps to the main square without the aid of the two or three single bulbs that were all the municipality could rise to. I was a newcomer to the village, staying for a few days in a small hotel on its far edge, just where the houses thinned out and the olive groves began; I had had no chance to become familiar with the walls, gradients and angles of the place; my feet could not go ahead of my eyes.

I have said that we were refugees from our black and rainy Northern nights, but when I got to the door I was greeted by a penetrating drizzle that might have been sighing in from the English Channel. When I had set out five hours earlier, the evening had been still and warm; I was wearing only light clothes. Laughing again, holding the episode firmly on a plateau of good humour, my hosts produced a large umbrella. I was dry, I was secure, the rainy cobbles were winking cheerfully in the stripes of yellow light from door and window: our parting words were said again, a few final small jokes produced a few complacent laughs, and I was on my way, with the door closing behind me.

In a diminutive tent of dry air, I went down the cobbled stairs with a high wall on one side of me and a wooden fence on the other. All around, the villagers slept, their bones laid out in easy patterns, their flesh heaped softly, their brains drinking in sleep like the roots of flowers after a shower of reviving rain. I thought of their impossibly hard lives, of their back-breaking work in this landscape of stones, roots and the hooves of mules. I thought of the harsh sunlight, so attractive in the travel folders, that puts wrinkles round their eyes and an eternal thirstiness in their flesh. And just as the thought came to me, I set foot on a fresh step ... and found myself in a universe of blackness. Jesus had switched the lights off.

I stopped dead, thinking fast, 'Your brain,' I said to myself, loudly, 'is your chief asset.' 'That is true,' I replied submissively. 'Then use it,' I commanded.

I moved to the left, extending my hand palm outwards. There was the wall. Now, forward and down. Holding the umbrella at a slight angle because of my closeness to the wall, I began to move.

One step. Two. Three. I estimated that there were about fifteen to go. But as I counted fourteen, my left hand was suddenly empty. The wall had ended abruptly in a corner. I was in the square.

Was there *no* light? No candle in an upper window? No insomniac citizen leaning over a balcony smoking a cigarette? I looked up, narrowing my eyelids against the soft wash of raindrops. No rift in the clouds that would show, suddenly, a cheerful scatter of stars?

Evidently not. The village was asleep and the night was firmly blanketed by this cool, strangling rain cloud. Under a full moon, it would doubtless have been a magic, luminous mist. But this night was moonless. I felt in my pocket for matches, knowing in advance that, as a non-smoker, I never carried them.

Nothing.

For a moment I was ready to weaken, to feel my way back to those steps, to knock on my friends' door and borrow an electric torch. Call in, somehow, the aid of that precious technology! But, at the thought, something archaic in me stiffened: some primitive, atavistic wish to prove myself an effective animal, to pit my resourcefulness against the elements. To go back for a flashlight – it seemed, suddenly, the typical modern capitulation, the action of a twentieth-century man, unable to live without his air-conditioning, his canned foods, sedatives and transistor radio.

No! Here I was, a man, with all a man's quickness and range of mind, a man's patience and adaptability, faced with a journey of no more than half a mile, over ground I had covered before. Only two or three times, it was true, and with no thought of studying the route. But enough, surely, for *homo sapiens*, the most successful of earth's creatures, clothed, erect, and in his right mind. And I remembered, further, that when I had asked the hotel people for a key before coming out, they had replied, all smiles, that the front door was never locked. There were no thieves in the village, no nocturnal intruders: honestidad! They had repeated the word, smiling in delight at the thought of the inviolable probity of their neighbours and themselves. Honestidad! The word came back to me and made me feel secure and confident.

Standing motionless in that softly hissing blackness, I took stock of my position. I knew I had to get across the square, and I found that my memory could reproduce its features clearly enough. I knew that the church occupied most of one side – a side to be avoided because of the flight of steps that jutted out and might be awkward to negotiate. On the other side were the bank and the post office, neither of which had steps. Directly facing me, I calculated, was the café, where I had stopped for a drink at noon that day. My best way would be to go round the square on the bank and post office side, keeping the wall within reach, until I could identify the café by its large plate-glass window; once there, I could find the narrow way that led, between blank walls, to my hotel at the edge of the village.

So I stood there, calculating, under my large umbrella. And suddenly I was shaken by laughter – I heard my own startling guffaw ring out in that tomblike calm. 'An old woman,' I said aloud, and laughed again. 'Standing here like an old woman!' And, despising myself for being so canny, I set off, walking straight in front of me. All I had to do was to cross one small village square – perhaps thirty yards!'

Daring the blackness to swallow me, I walked for five confident, swinging, sightless paces.

One, two, three, four, five ... and terror and pain crashed into me simultaneously. The hardness of metal banged into me, the emptiness of air giddied me, the torment of loneliness grabbed at me, panic squeezed my chest. My umbrella skidded away and was lost. I stood back, cursing, rubbing. The panic receded, but still I was humiliated, knowing myself beaten, an object of pity to myself and to the impersonal universe.

In plain language, I had walked into a car.

There had been no cars in the square during the day-time. Plenty of wheeled traffic was about in the district, but the square had been given over entirely to pedestrians – in consequence, I had vaguely supposed, of some regulation. And now! At midnight, with Jesus in bed, with no help forthcoming from anywhere, somebody had to leave his accursed car ... Some Jack-in-Office, or the cousin of the mayor, or just someone with a little money, above the reach of the village regulations ... But why *one* car? How did I know there weren't half a dozen?

My shin felt numb: perhaps it was broken. The pain in my elbow was less agonizing, but still bad enough. More important, where was my umbrella? I no longer wanted it as a protection from the rain – in my state of misery, wetness was a detail too small to be noticed. But, once closed, it could be used as a walking stick. It, and nothing else, could save me from a recurrence of this shattering impact. I longed for it with a wild, desperate longing. What had happened? In the instant of the collision, I had unclenched my hand, and the umbrella had skated across the car's smooth metal roof. It would be easy enough, surely, to ... I felt my way round to the other side of the car. Down here, on the ground, somewhere. I bent down and groped. Nothing. I moved away from the car, stooped, and felt the wet paving stones in front of me, behind me, on each side ... where was the car?

Terrified, I scuttled back to it and stood with one hand resting on its roof. I had to know where I was. If I lost my bearings, I might walk into the car again, and another accident would finish me.

Where was that bloody umbrella?

Keeping one hand on the car, I bent down and swept my free arm round in a wide, inquiring circle. Nothing. I got down and lay flat on the ground, face down, with my hand firmly gripping a tyre. Then I inched round in a slow rotation. My belly dragged across the wet stone; my shirt was sopping. Then my ankle touched something. The umbrella! I jack-knifed upward and grabbed. Safe! I had it!

Restored, equipped, confident, I stood up. One decisive movement closed the umbrella, a second brought it into contact with the ground. Tap, tap. The sound was a benediction. It was the sound of reason, the voice of the mind.

Playfully now, I reached out and knocked on the car. Tinny beast. It had bruised my flesh and threatened to break my bones, but it could not hurt the steel and whale-bone of the umbrella. Mastery!

I cackled aloud at the thought of my advantage. I could even take revenge on the brute who had left his car in the darkness. Grinning, the umbrella tucked firmly under my arm, I bent down and unscrewed the valve of the nearest tyre. It sighed and flattened; the car canted over slightly. 'I'll teach him,' I panted, and stood back, satisfied. But where did that leave me? Was I still on the side of the car I had bumped into, or had I worked my way round to the other side? Was the café in front of me, the post office on my right, the church on my left, or vice versa?

I opened my eyes wide and swivelled my head round. Not a trace of light. I might have been in a mine-shaft: the world was closed in, wrapped round in black velvet. My eyes were useless. Only my hands could help me.

Gripping the umbrella, tapping it restlessly on the ground in front of me, I moved straight ahead. Or so I thought. But when the umbrella finally came up against one of the walls that bounded the square, my shoulder rubbed it almost as soon as the stick tapped it. I must have come at it not frontally, as I expected, but obliquely.

Never mind, I had it. All I had to do now was to feel my way until I felt the steps of the church. Then I should be able to reassemble, from its now scattered elements, my picture of the square. Then to the café – then to the alleyway – and soon, to the comfort of dry clothes, sheets and pillow, safety!

Slowly I tapped along the wall. It seemed to take hours. Then a right-angled corner came within the purview of the umbrella. Obediently, I turned. Tap, tap, tap, slowly now along this wall. Where could I be? I felt with my hand, but recognized nothing. I went as slowly as a beetle. Another right-angle in the wall, brusquely turning aside the busy antenna I presented to it. Tap, tap. I was gaining in confidence. Two walls down, only two to come, and surely one of them would . . . the earth rushed up to meet me, my foot was too far back to take my weight, a knee shot forward and was cruelly punished. I rolled. Savage blows beat the air from my lungs. Grimly, through it all, I held on to the umbrella. I might die, but if so I would be found holding on to the handle.

Sprawled on the church steps I lay, trying to decide which pain was worse, the one in my kneecap or the one in my ribs. I was smashed, ruined, an old man in wet clothes, where five hours before I had been a young dandy stepping out to a social evening. And, amid all my misery, the indefatigable reasoning process was deducing, arguing, working out what had happened.

Yes. The church had a broad, shallow step, followed by a flight of narrower ones. The swinging tip of my umbrella had missed the lowest step, and my foot had caught against it in mid-stride, throwing my body forward on to the sharp steps beyond. Undoubtedly, that was it. My skull, at any rate, was unbroken: my brain was clear.

At least I knew, now, where I was. The café, with my alleyway at the side of it, was behind me. I had gone past them in my diligent beetle-walk round the square.

Taking a firm grip on the umbrella, I went back the way I had come. Here was the wall, here was the corner, and this smooth surface must be the plate-glass front of the café. Was my knee bleeding? I felt my leg, but it was so wet from the rain that an extra wetness of blood would not have been noticed. Still, it hurt when I put any weight on that leg. And my side ached furiously. No matter, I could move, and as long as life continued I would keep moving. To die crawling towards an objective – that was the great human attribute.

My left hand clutched emptiness. I stopped, explored, stroked the corner of the building with my thumb. Yes, this was the alleyway. I had found the way: I was free to leave the square! 'I'm coming,' I breathed excitedly. 'I'm on my way – on my way – '

A galvanized iron bucket rang sharply against the umbrella's ferrule. Aha! Thought you'd trip me again, did you? I kicked it over, skilfully aiming so as to send it bounding away in a series of oval jumps. It seemed loud enough to wake the whole village, and for a moment I hoped it would, hoped that yellow squares of light would suddenly stand out in all the high walls that I knew were near to me. Then I remembered: Jesus was off duty. The best I could hope for was the slow climbing flame of a candle here and there. And who, turning over in his soft bed, was going to get up and hunt for matches?

Holding to the wall, tapping the ground ahead of me, I made a smart three miles an hour for perhaps twenty yards. Then bang! Another bucket. What was this mania for leaving buckets outside their houses? I stooped and picked this one up, then threw it over a wall. I heard a wet smack, as if it had landed on a flower-bed. My luck again. I was hoping to break something. I wanted to pass on some of my suffering to the snoring villagers, to let them feel how much I resented their hard stones and unpredictable angles, their cruel motor-cars, murderous church steps, ambushing buckets.

Then the wall ended. I moved crabwise across the road and tried the other side. That, too, was open. I was on my own.

I went forward, tapping. As long as I could hear the metalled surface of the road, I was all right. But how far was the road metalled? I had hardly noticed as I blithely strolled along it in the evening sunshine, but now I distinctly remembered that for some distance before it reached my hotel, the road gave up its macadam and became a rough, stony track. I could still feel my way along it, but only step by step: the short parched grass at the roadside, sprinkled with stones and bare patches, wouldn't sound very different from the roadway. I was still wrestling with this thought when I walked into the lower branches of a tree. I halted, and backed. No harm done. But my heart was pounding with fear.

'Come on,' I said to myself. 'Think of birds flying across oceans.' I thought of them, but my heart refused to slow down. The night seemed, suddenly, to be full of life – alien, watchful, malignant life. Monstrous fancies struggled for birth in my mind. For one brief moment I saw – yes, actually *saw* with the violent accuracy of the inner eye – an animal about to attack me: a huge moose, dark red in colour, with baleful yellow eyes. Why a moose, I don't know; a wolf or a bear, or even a tiger, would have seemed more natural in this southern landscape: but fantasies aren't natural, and the animal I saw glowering at me out of that darkness was a colossal moose.

I clung to the branches of the tree, which suddenly seemed friendly and sheltering, and – absurdly enough – I covered my eyes and waited for the moose to go away. After a moment, it vanished, and I slowly let go of the tree. My umbrella reassured me with its solid weight and its normality. Tap, tap. I began again. This was the road. That tree must have been at the left-hand verge. I took three crab-steps right. Good. Now forward.

I tapped along for some forty paces before lurching down into the ditch on the other side. I climbed out, feeling with the palm of my hand for the hard stones of the roadway. I was beginning to shiver, partly from tension and partly from effort and fatigue. Once again I forced myself to think steadily. I *wasn't* lost in the jungle, there *weren't* any wild animals about, nobody was going to shoot at me with a poisoned blowpipe. I was simply on the outskirts of a peaceful village in a civilized European country, on a night when a low veil of rain clouds happened to have blotted out the stars. What was more, I was within a hundred yards of my hotel – somewhere over to my right and up a short gravel path. Shelter, calm, a warm bed. I *must* get there. I was ready to do *anything* to cheat this hideous blackness. Grimly I went down on my hands and knees and began to crawl along the road's edge, keeping my right hand on the grass verge, my left on the road.

The rain was falling more heavily now, striking directly on to my back and soaking through my thin jacket. My damaged kneecap gave an agonizing stab every time it came into contact with the road, but when I tried straightening my knees and lumbering along with my body arched into a stiff semicircle, the muscular effort caused my bruised ribs such violent pain that I dropped to my knees again. My fear, at least, had gone. It seemed to me, in that farcical desperation, that I had nothing left to fear.

Abruptly, my right hand felt the prickle of gravel. For a moment I kept motionless. Was this the beginning of my deliverance, or just another horrible disappointment? I lifted the hand and put it down again a little further on. Yes! Gravel! I filled my hands, both of them, and threw the pebbles down: they made a crisp, scattering noise, as melodious to my ears as a chime of bells.

Feverishly I scrambled to my feet and tested the theory that this was, in fact, the path leading up to my hotel. It went up at the proper angle. It was bordered with rank grass: I could feel the thin stalks in my fingers. It climbed. I tested it step by step. I poked into the darkness with my umbrella. The ferrule hit what was unmistakably a wall. I took another step and laid my hand flat on the wall. It was real. I was saved.

Here was the door. Heavy oak, with iron studs and a circular iron handle. All that, and they leave it unlocked! Honestidad. Well, I was grateful for it. To get inside, to go up the stairs to a soft bed and dry pyjamas! – already, the adventure was turning into something amusing, something to make a good story when I saw my friends again.

I pushed the door open. The darkness inside couldn't have been any denser than that outside, but the stillness, the sense of enclosure, made it seem as if I were in a tomb. I remembered, nervously, that I wasn't sure which room was mine. I knew it was on the first floor, but was it the second door along or the third? At the thought of blundering into the bedroom of a sleeping Spaniard, I quailed: I was on the point of deciding to sit quietly on the stairs until dawn broke, when I remembered that I had another sense which, so far, had been no use to me that night. I could *hear*. If I opened the door very carefully, millimetre by millimetre, my ears would soon tell me if there was a sound of breathing coming from the bed.

Arms outstretched, I went towards where I knew the stairs were. One step, two, three, and suddenly I was in trouble again. My knee hit something hard and yet spidery. I clutched. Then I was down, clawing, amid a tangle of bars and a gentle whirring and ticking.

A bicycle!

Sweating, I disengaged myself and felt for the wall to steady me. What kind of a hotel was it that allowed people to leave bicycles in the hallway at night? I bent down to pick up the still ticking machine. But just as I moved, a voice very close to me said, calmly:

'Buenas tardes.'

My heart nearly stopped. Not that there was anything alarming about the voice, as such. It was calm and level, and only slightly inquiring. But I was so utterly attuned to silence and loneliness, so absorbed in my private battle with the universe, that the sound of a human voice, close to my ear, was the most startling sound I could possibly have heard.

'Who is it?' I said sharply. Then, realizing that whoever it was probably didn't understand English, I tried to think of the Spanish for 'Who is it,' but I was too flustered, and after a pause I said, lamely, 'Dispense usted.' That's good, I thought, asking him to excuse me when he's just frightened me almost into a fit!

There was a silence. I decided to carry on in such Spanish as

I had, so I haltingly translated my simple phrases before uttering them. The conversation went like this:

'Where are you?'

'In the parlour.'

'Excuse me for your bicycle.'

(A gentle laugh.) 'It is not my bicycle.'

'Excuse me for the noise. I want to find my room.'

'Your room?' There was a short pause, and then the voice said, 'You have no room here, señor.'

I was about to make an impatient reply when the truth crashed into my brain. *Wrong house!*

'Hotel Miramar?' I faltered.

'The next house. Fifty metres.'

'My God,' I said. 'Forgive me. Excuse me. *Sírvase usted! Gracias! Buenas noches. Hasta la vista. Adiós. Medianoche. Sírvase. Adiós.*' I was backing fast now, feeling behind me for the door, dodging the accursed bicycle.

'Stay,' said the voice. 'Sit down in the parlour.' Then came a sentence or two I couldn't understand.

'*No comprendo,*' I said.

The voice repeated the words and I caught one I recognized. '*Alba.*' Dawn! I turned my head this way and that, searching for a window. Then I saw it. I was standing by an open door leading off the hallway. The room had a large window, and through it I saw that the sky outside was no longer black.

'*Luz,*' I said. 'Light.' The words were beautiful. I went on through the only other languages I knew a smattering of. '*Lux. Lumière.*' The words themselves were an expression of thanks: humanity's gratitude to the Creator for bringing the day back every twenty-four hours.

Then it struck me what a strange situation I was in. If I had not been so dazed, I should have asked myself long ago what this man was doing. All right, it was his own house, or at any rate he lived in it. But why was he lurking in the pitch blackness, downstairs, when he might have been sleeping in his bed? As the light grew, I became curious to see him. I took a pace or two into the room. But I could not locate him.

'*Dónde –* ' I was beginning when my hand brushed against his face. I drew back, thoroughly startled. He was sitting just inside the doorway. I apologized, and his firm, quiet voice assured me that there was no harm done. Leaning back against the wall, I waited. The windowpanes were a light grey in the room. Pools and bars of blackness began to stand out in the general blackness.

I saw my interlocutor. He was sitting very still, upright, in a wooden armchair. He was fully dressed and his head was turned attentively towards me as if he were watching my face.

Only, of course, he was not watching my face.

'Usted . . .' I stammered. '*Ciego?*'

I saw him nod, gently. 'Blind. Since the fighting.'

I saw him now clearly. He was about fifty, strongly built, with thick, greying hair neatly brushed, and powerful square hands lying on the wooden arms of his chair. I wanted to speak to him, to tell him that I understood the tragedy that had befallen him, that I regretted the fighting, that I was against all fighting. But when I opened my mouth all that came out was:

'*Gracias.*'

I don't know what I was thanking him for. Or perhaps it was the Creator I was thanking, or the fate that had spared my eyes, or just the light. He seemed to take it, quite simply, that I was thanking him for the shelter of the house, because he told me in his quiet, calm voice that I was welcome, and then said, as he heard me begin to shuffle out:

'*Buenas noshes.*'

'No,' I said. '*Buenos días.*' I could not leave without telling him that another day had begun.

He chuckled, as if I had made a small joke, and repeated, '*Buenos días.*'

Good day, I said to myself as I went out through the heavy oak door and stood at the top of the grassy slope. Good day, good day, good day, good day, good day.

The Valentine Generation

Quarter to eight on a Monday morning, well into April but still pretty fresh, and I'm off to a fair start with the collecting. I may be getting on towards retiring age, but I can still get round the boxes as quick as any of them and quicker than most. The secret is to get a move on in the early stages. Get round as many as you can by nine o'clock. After that, the traffic sets in heavy and slows you down so much that you can pretty well reckon to take double time over everything.

This morning I've got one of the light vans and it looks as if I'm getting away easy. I'm round the South-West Fifteen area, the other side of the river. Nice quiet suburban streets, with trees in fresh bloom. Like a trip to the country. So of course I let myself be lulled into feeling optimistic. Forty years with the Post Office and I *still* haven't got it into my head that trouble always hits you when you've got your guard down.

I'm coming up to the third box and even as I drive up to it I can see this girl standing there on the pavement. She's only a couple of yards away from the pillar-box, but my early warning system still doesn't go off: I think perhaps she's waiting for somebody to come out of one of the houses, some girl-friend she travels to work with or her little brother that she's seeing to school. Funny joke.

I get out of the van and go over to the box with my bunch of keys and my bag at the ready. And straight away I see that she's watching me. I try to take no notice, but her eyes are boring two holes in the back of my neck.

I open the box and there are the letters. Not many, because most people who post on a Sunday manage to catch the five o'clock collection. About a couple of dozen in all. I'm just sweeping them into the bag when the girl takes a step towards me. I see her out of the corner of my eye and I straighten up.

For a moment I wonder if I'm going to be coshed or something. There's a kind of desperation about her. But she's alone, a nice-looking girl, about twenty, good class, well dressed. She's very unhappy, I can see that. All stirred up about something. But it's no business of mine. On the collecting, you've no time to spare before nine o'clock. After that, you might just as well slacken off, that's what I always tell them.

I turn to go back to the van, but she's speaking to me. I don't quite catch what she's saying. She's too confused, the sounds just tumble out over one another.

'Anything wrong, Miss?' I say to her, but as I speak I'm opening the van door. She's not going to hold me up, whatever she wants.

'Yes,' she says. 'There's something terribly wrong. But you could put it right for me in a minute, if you'd be very kind.'

I don't like the sound of that, but she's waiting for me to say something, so I decide to give her one minute of my time. Just one minute. She's in trouble, and I've got daughters of my own.

'What is it I can do for you?' I say. 'It'd better be something I can do within sixty seconds, because on this job, it's all a question of how much you can do before nine – '

She doesn't let me finish. She's all over me, reaching out as if she wants to grab hold of my arm. 'You can, you can easily do it straight away,' she says. 'It's just that – I've posted a letter that I ought never to have posted. And I want to get it back. If it goes it'll do terrible harm that I could never do anything about. You will give it me, won't you? Please?'

It's a funny thing, but as I stand there listening to her I have a kind of 'This-is-where-I-came-in' feeling. All those years ago, when I first joined the Post Office, I used to wonder if anybody would ever come up to me when I was on collecting and ask me if they could have a letter back. And now at last it's happened. Of course I've always known I couldn't do it.

'Sorry, miss,' I say, shaking my head. 'Firmest rule in the book. Once a thing's posted, it's in the care of the Post Office until it reaches the party it's addressed to.'

She draws a deep breath and I can see she's getting ready to work hard. 'Look,' she begins. But I'm too quick for her. 'No, you look,' I say to her. 'Forty years I've worked for the Post

Office, and all through those forty years it's been my living. A job to do, a wage, pension at the end of it, social club, met most of my friends through it one way and another. It's like being married. Forty years and you don't even want a change. You find you can't even imagine it any more.'

'Being married!' she says, gulping, as if I'd said something that really hurt her. 'I wouldn't know. I've never been married yet, and if you're going to stand on those regulations of yours and refuse to give just one little letter back, just *once* in forty years, I don't suppose I ever shall be.'

It's not that I'm heartless, but at that I just have to laugh. 'Oh, come *on*,' I say to her. 'A pretty young thing like you. Never married, that's a laugh!'

'Oh, you're so clever,' she says, sad and angry at the same time. 'You know everything, don't you? All right, probably if my entire happiness is ruined, I'll get over it one day, enough to marry somebody just for the sake of having a normal life and a family. But I shan't be happy.'

'We've all had it,' I said. 'Nobody in the world's good enough except just one person.'

'Don't you believe in love?' she asks.

'Well, as a matter of fact I do,' I say. 'I got married myself, soon after I joined the Post Office, and I can't believe I'd have been so happy with anyone else as I have with my wife. I did all right when I picked her out. But that was back in the days when marriages were made to last. Everything's different with you young people today.'

'You think so?' she says. 'Really different?'

'Course it is,' I say. 'All the romance has gone out of it. Well, look at it. Sex, sex, sex from morning to night and never a bit of sentiment.'

'What's wrong with sex?' she says, looking stubborn.

'Nothing,' I say, 'only in my day we didn't try to build a fire with nothing but kindling.'

I turn away, thinking I'll leave her to chew that one over. I'm just getting the van door open when suddenly she's there, grabbing at my wrist.

'Please,' she says. '*Please*. You've got a kind face. I know you'd help me if only you knew.'

'Well, I haven't got time to know,' I say, trying to get free. 'I thought you said it would be sixty seconds.'

'I wrote a letter to the man I'm in love with,' she says, speaking very quickly and holding on to my wrist. 'A horrible, hurtful letter telling him I didn't want any more to do with him, and saying a lot of horrible things that weren't even true. Things I just made up to try to hurt him – to make him suffer.'

'And now you're sorry for him,' I say. 'Well, write him another letter and tell him it was all a pack of lies.'

'You don't understand,' she says. 'It isn't that I'm sorry for him, it's just that I want him back. And he'll never, *never* come back to me if he reads that letter. He'll never forgive me.'

'He will if he loves you,' I say.

'Oh, it's hopeless,' she says with a kind of groan. 'You talk as if love was so simple.'

'Well, so it is,' I tell her. 'If two people love each other, they want to be nice, and help each other, and make things easy. I know there are lovers' quarrels, but they're soon patched up. Why, that's all part of the fun of being in love. You'll find out when the real thing comes along.'

'The real thing!' she groans again. 'I tell you this is the real thing, all the way through. Look, why don't you believe me and let me take my letter back?'

'I've told you why,' I say. 'Forty years with the Post Office and you want me to start ignoring regulations?'

'All right,' she says, speaking very low and looking at me fiercely. 'Go ahead and keep your regulations. But think about it sometimes in the middle of the night. How you sacrificed somebody's happiness for the whole of their life, rather than break a regulation.'

'I've told you before, you're being silly,' I say. 'Look, I'll prove it to you. Number one, you don't really love this bloke.'

'Don't love him!' she wails. 'How can you possibly tell that?'

'Well, does it look like it?' I say. 'You get your rag out about something, and straight away you write him such a stinking letter, full of insults and things that aren't even true, that you daren't go near him once he reads it.'

'That doesn't prove I don't love him,' she says. 'All it proves is that I was desperate. Look, let me tell you what happened.'

84

'All right,' I say, 'but make it fast. And don't kid yourself that I'll give you the letter when you've finished.' I meant it, too. Regulations mean a lot after forty years.

'I usually spend Saturday evening with Jocelyn,' she begins. *Jocelyn.* I don't like the sound of that. 'And last Saturday, that's the day before yesterday, he rings up and tells me he can't do it. He's got to look after his aunt who's coming up from the country. So when my brother and sister-in-law happened to look in and see me, I said I'd go out with them for the evening. We went up to the West End and I said I'd show them a nice little restaurant I know. So we went into this place and the very first person I saw was Jocelyn.'

'With his aunt from the country,' I say.

'With his aunt from the country,' she says, nodding and looking very grim. 'About twenty years old with a lot of red hair and a dress cut very low. And there was Jocelyn, leaning towards her the way he does when he's really interested in a girl.'

'What a surprise for him,' I say.

'No surprise,' she says. 'He never saw me. I knew at once I wouldn't be able to stand it. I wasn't going to have a showdown with him there and then, and as for sitting down and watching the performance and trying to eat my dinner, with my brother and his wife there on top of everything else, well.'

'So you ducked out quick, and came home and wrote him a nasty letter,' I say. Nine o'clock's creeping up and I'm ruddy nowhere with my collecting.

'If only I could have come straight home,' she says. 'But I have my brother and his wife to cope with. He's always saying I can't look after myself. I wasn't going to talk about it to him. So I looked round quickly and said sorry, this was the wrong place and I'd made a mistake. They said it looked all right and they'd like to try it anyway, but I said no, I was so keen to show them this special place. So there we were, out in the street, with them waiting for me to guide them and me with no idea where to go. We wandered about for ages, and my brother was in a filthy temper, and then I took them into a place and pretended that was it and it was awful. Oh, it was all so utterly, utterly awful I couldn't even talk. I could only say yes and no

85

when they seemed to expect me to say something. I expect they thought I was mad.'

'So after *that* you wrote him a letter,' I say, trying to move her along even though the collections have now gone for a dead Burton.

'After that,' she says, 'I go home and spend a completely sleepless night. I don't even close my eyes, because every time I close them I see Jocelyn's face as he leans towards this girl.'

'All right, let him lean,' I say. 'If he's the type that runs after every bit of skirt he sees, he won't make you happy anyway.'

'But he *does* make me happy,' she says. 'He's absolutely ideal for me. He makes me feel marvellous. When I'm with him I'm really glad about being a woman.'

'Even if you can't trust him?' I ask.

'Casual infidelities don't matter,' she says. 'It's the really deep communication between a man and woman that matters.'

I can see this is getting out of my league altogether, so I make one more effort to brush her off. 'All right,' I say. 'If your Jocelyn is in the deep-communication business, he won't be put off by a nasty letter. He'll see straight away that you only wrote it because you were angry or desperate or whatever it is.'

'You're wrong,' she says, looking at me very steadily. 'There are some insults a man can't forgive. Listen, I wrote that letter on Sunday afternoon. I'd been crying nearly all morning, and every time I sat down to write I was just crying too much to see the paper. By the time I got down to it I was feeling murderous. I wrote things that I knew he'd find absolutely unforgivable. I laughed at him, I told him he hadn't been adequate for me, that I'd had other lovers all the time we'd been together. I must have been mad. I wrote so many details he'll never believe it isn't true.'

'You say you love him?' I ask.

'I love him and need him utterly,' she says.

'Rubbish,' I say. The whole thing is beginning to get me down. 'If that's love, so is a boxing match. It's just vanity and sex, that's all it is. There's no love anywhere.'

'Well, perhaps that's not a bad definition,' she says, as if I've got all day to stand there and discuss it. 'I mean, one's need for another person is partly vanity isn't it? It's all bound up with one's own belief in oneself.'

'One this and one that,' I say. 'You're just hair-splitting. If you love anybody, you care for them, don't you? You want them to be happy.'

'That's a chocolate-box idea of love,' she says. 'I mean it's not what happens when real people get involved with each other. You may have been able to live your life by those ideas, but in that case you've been very lucky. You've never had to face reality.'

Reality! From a chit of a girl like this I'm learning about reality!

'Oh, I'm sure you've had lots of reality in your life,' she says. 'I know you've had all sorts of responsibilities and everything. It's just that your personal relations must have been unreal. You wouldn't talk about love in that sort of Royal Doulton way if they hadn't been.'

All at once I understand. She's not giving me her own opinions. She's just parroting what this Jocelyn's been teaching her. Deep communication between man and woman! I can just see his idea of it. Especially if he's got her trained so that she doesn't even count the other girls he runs after. And Royal Doulton! That's not the sort of thing she'd think up for her-self.

'Listen to me, miss,' I say. 'Take an old man's advice and leave that letter where it is. If it puts an end to this business between you and this Jocelyn bloke, believe me, you'll live to be grate-ful.'

At that she stares at me as if she's caught me doing some-thing so horrible she can't trust her own eyesight.

'It's unbelievable,' she says at last. 'If anybody had told me that – that ordinary human beings were capable of such stupidity and cruelty, yes, *cruelty*, I wouldn't have believed them.' And she begins to cry, quite silently, with the tears running down her nose.

'Which of us is cruel?' I ask her. 'Me, or Jocelyn?'

'You, of course,' she says, so cross at what she thinks is cheek on my part that she stops crying. 'You're making me miserable *for ever* just so that you won't have to admit that your ideas about love are out of date and wrong.'

'Whereas Jocelyn is sweetness and kindness itself, eh?' I put in.

'No, of course not,' she says. 'He's capable of hardness and aggressiveness and he can be cruel himself at times. That's all part of his being a real man, the sort of man who can make a girl feel good about being feminine.' That's another bit of Jocelyn's patter, if I'm any judge. 'A man who was *sweetness and kindness itself*,' she goes on, bringing out the words as if they're choking her, 'wouldn't be capable of making a woman feel fulfilled and happy. He's got to have a streak of – of – '

'Of the jungle in him?' I say, trying to help her out.

'If you like, yes,' she says, nodding and looking solemn.

'Well, I don't like,' I say, letting it rip for once. 'I think you're a nice girl, but you're being very silly. You've let this Jocelyn stuff your head full of silly ideas, you've taken his word for it that he can chase every bit of skirt he meets, tell lies to you, string you along every inch of the way, and it all doesn't matter because he's going to make you feel happy and relaxed, he's Tarzan of the flipping Apes. No, listen to me,' I tell her, because I can see she's trying to stick her oar in, 'I've stood here and listened to your story and made myself so late that the collections won't be right for the whole of today, and now I'm going to tell you what you ought to do. You're a nice girl. Cut this Jocelyn out of your life like the rotten thing he is. Go and find some young man who'll tell you that as a woman you deserve to be cherished and taken care of. Who'll love you enough to tell you the truth and play fair with you. Even if he isn't an animal out of the Zoo. Make do with an ordinary human being,' I say to her. 'You'll find it cheaper in the long run.'

Instead of answering, she just stands there crying. All right, I think to myself, let her get on with it. I've given her the right advice and that's the end.

I get into the van and press the self-starter. I'd left the engine running but it doesn't idle fast enough on these crisp mornings, and it'd stalled. So anyway, I start it up and I'm just going to engage gear and move off when, for some reason, I can't do it. My foot comes off the accelerator and I look out of the window. There she is, still crying. Now's your cue to call me a sentimental old fool.

So I get out of the van again and I go back to where she's standing, crying her eyes out.

'Look, miss,' I say, 'It's the best thing, you know. He wouldn't have been any good to you.'

'Why ...' she begins, but she's crying too much to talk. I wait a bit and she has another go and this time it comes out. 'Why are you so sure that you know best and that I must be wrong?' she asks me.

'Well, it's simple,' I say. 'I've had a happy marriage for nearly forty years. So naturally I know how they work. I know what you have to do.'

'But love *changes*!' she says, bringing it out as if she's struggling for words that'll convince me. 'I'm sure you've been happy, but you're wrong if you think that your way of being happy would work for young people of today. You belong to a different generation.'

'And that makes me not human?' I ask. 'Look, I've been happy with May for forty years and we've had three children. That's not done without love.'

'Your kind of love,' she says. 'Your generation's kind. I'll bet you used to send each other Valentines with sentimental rhymes on them.'

That gets my rag out. 'Yes, so we damn well did,' I say. 'And not only that. We used to give one another keepsakes. Listen, the first time we ever went for a walk in the country, when we were courting, I picked some flowers for May and she took them home and pressed them between the leaves of a book – *and she's got them today*! Can you understand that? I wanted to love her and take care of her because she was a woman – that was the way I made her feel good, not telling her a lot of stuff about deep communication and keeping one eye out for the next little piece that came in sight. Valentines!' I say, and I must be speaking quite loud, because some people on the other side of the road stop and stare at me, 'yes, we sent each other Valentines, big ones made of lace paper, shaped like hearts, some of 'em.

89

That's something else you wouldn't understand. Try talking to Jocelyn about hearts!'

That's done it. I've got carried away and now I'm as upset as she is. I'm about ready to burst out crying myself. And me forty years with the Post Office. At this rate nobody'll get any letters at all.

'You think I don't know what love is, don't you?' the girl says. 'You're quite sure that whatever I feel for Jocelyn, it's not love.'

'Not what I'd call love,' I tell her. 'But you've got to excuse me. I don't know what love's supposed to be nowadays. I come from the wrong generation.'

'The Valentine generation,' she says and all of a sudden she's smiling at me, yes, *smiling*.

'Weren't there women in your generation,' she says, 'who loved men and went on loving them even if they didn't treat them right? Didn't they sometimes love husbands who got drunk or stayed away all night?'

'I've known the type,' I say.

'And what did you think about them?' she goes on. 'Did you think they were just fools who didn't know what they were doing?'

'That was different,' I say. 'A woman might go on loving a husband who mistreated her. But at least she didn't say that she loved him *because* he mistreated her. She loved him in *spite* of it.'

'Are you sure?' she says. 'Was it always as clear as that just why she loved him?'

'What are you getting at?' I ask.

'I'm trying to get you to admit,' she says, 'that other people might know what love is besides you.'

'I'm quite sure they do,' I say. 'All I'm telling you is that you're wrong if you think you love this Jocelyn. You can't love a man who brings you so low.'

'And you're not even going to let me try,' she says, not crying now but just looking steadily into my face.

'Look,' I say, just to finish it. 'Let's have a bargain. You tell me what you think love is, and if I agree with you I'll give you your letter back.'

'Just that?' she says. 'Just tell you what I think love is?'

'Yes,' I say. I'm quite certain that whatever she says it'll be Jocelyn's angle.

'And you'll give me the letter back?' she says.

'If I agree with what you say, yes,' I say.

'Well,' she says, without even stopping to think, 'It's – wanting to be with somebody all the time.'

'All the time? You're sure?' I ask her.

'It's wanting to wake up with the same person every morning and do everything together and tell each other everything,' she says.

'You know that, do you?' I say.

'Yes,' she says. 'I know that.'

I go over to the van and get the bag out. If anybody sees this, I can be sacked, forty years or no forty years. But there's hardly anybody about, and a bargain's a bargain.

'I'll be very quick,' she says, rummaging away. She shuffles the envelopes like a pack of cards and in no time at all she's found her letter and it's away, safe and sound, in her handbag.

'Bless you,' she says. 'I knew you'd want to help me really.'

'I did want to help you,' I say, 'and I still think I'd have helped you more if I'd hung on to that letter.'

'Don't worry about me,' she says, smiling.

'Just tell me one thing,' I say as I'm opening the van door. 'Your idea of love. Would you say it was the same as Jocelyn's?'

'No,' she says, as chirpy as a sparrow. 'It's quite different.'

'What's going to happen, then,' I ask her, 'if you've both got different ideas about love?'

'I'll take care of that,' she says. I can see she's not worried at all. 'It's what I feel for him that matters, not what he feels for me. I just want him around, that's all.'

I get into the van and this time I drive away. The collections are up a big, tall gum tree. I have plenty of time stuck in traffic jams and I keep thinking of her and Jocelyn. How she doesn't care what he is or what he thinks or even what he *does*, so long as she has him. Doesn't sound like happiness to me. But all at once, the thought comes to me, well, she'll probably get what she wants. I mean to say, it didn't take her long to get me to break a Post Office regulation I'd never broken in forty years. She twisted me round her little finger, so it could be she'll twist him.

But then, of course, I'm soft-hearted compared with a chap like that. The Valentine generation. I wonder what May'd say. Not that I'll ever know. There are some things a man keeps to himself. 'Was she pretty?' I can just hear her asking. 'Must have been, for you to stand there talking to her and get behind with your collections and finish up with risking the sack, and no provision for our old age.' No, the only way to get an idea would be to imagine May at that girl's age. She was a real woman. Not much Royal Doulton there.

I wonder.

Further Education

It doesn't take much to raise a ghost. This one was raised by the voice of my secretary saying, 'I thought I'd better put this letter aside for you to look at personally, Mr Richards. It doesn't look like a thing that could go through the ordinary routine of the firm.'

At that, I knew at once that something special, and probably irritating and/or money-losing, was coming my way. The firm's routines are pretty inclusive ones – I've seen to that – and anything that can't be absorbed by them means trouble, as a rule. But this wasn't trouble. Just a ghost. And I don't believe in ghosts, so why should I worry?

Dear James [the letter said],

It must be all of twenty years since we met, though I must say our undergraduate days seem only yesterday to me. Perhaps that is the result of being continuously in the same surroundings, having stayed in Oxford all through the years and, indeed, at the same College. I don't recall having seen you at College reunions or celebrations of any kind, though of course these events are apt to be tiresome, and are avoided by many men who look back quite kindly on their student years and the associations that date from them. I hope this is the case with you, because I have a request to make, and, if you don't remember our earlier contact with some sort of pleasure, it is bound to seem an intrusion . . .

Not a bad opening for a begging letter, eh? Plenty of dignity, a good selling line, a handshake that wasn't a backslap at the same time. (I could use that man!) I'd looked at the end of the letter, of course, to see the name before I started to read it. But even if I hadn't, I'd have known by the end of the first paragraph. Poor old Gerard. Bill Gerard, the one man I'd met at Oxford who could truly be called a scholar and a gentleman. In my own case, as I freely admitted, I'd gone up to Oxford to have a good time and make a few contacts; I never made the slightest attempt to be a scholar, and though I can be a gentleman when I want to, I don't always want to. That's why, after twenty years, he was writing begging letters to me, instead of the other way round.

After two decades of sitting still at Oxford, I am about to take a plunge into what seems, to me, the world of action. There is a big educational scheme afoot in East Africa, and I am going out there to play what part I can in it.

I skipped the next bit, just glancing over it and getting a name here and a figure there. Just like Bill Gerard to get all starry-eyed about a scheme for educating black savages. I could see him, standing up there and talking about Plato to a lot of stark-naked buck Africans pretending to listen while actually they were wondering what his liver would taste like, fried or grilled. So that was the magnet that was drawing him away from his comfortable nest in Oxford – the fool. I felt the blood rising to my face with annoyance, the same annoyance I feel when these fools come round trying to bleed me white for these crazy schemes like 'war on want'. Good God, they just can't see beyond the ends of their noses. Suppose they do succeed – which they won't – in stamping out the hunger and disease these Africans and Asians live in. What then? As soon as they're not hungry any more, they work better, they dress in good clothes, they pick up skills. Next thing, they're running their own industries and it's 'White man, get out.' Every time one of these damned interfering fools signs a cheque for another truckload of food and medicines for some benighted part of the earth, they're carving another slice off the market that keeps *them* alive. War on want! Once you get rid of their want we'll have war all right. Economic war to the knife. I never argue with these people, mind you. All you can do in this world is look after your own interests and let 'em get on with it.

So here was old Bill Gerard, coming back into my life after twenty years, asking me for money to set him up on a lecture platform in East Africa, talking about Plato to chaps with filed teeth. And the only thing I could think of was, What about Hazel? How will she fit into East Africa?

I called my secretary over, and was just going to dictate some kind of polite brush-off, when suddenly a wild idea struck me. I wanted to see Hazel again. Yes, even Bill. It would amuse me to take a look at him too. They say you oughtn't to revisit your past, but I don't know.

So I went straight ahead and dictated a personal letter to Bill suggesting that I call at his house one week-end and discuss the possibility of contributing to his African fund. He replied, and that was that. Sunday lunch at his house in North Oxford. I brushed off any suggestion of taking Liz and the kids along for the trip. Told them it was business. I told Evans to bring the car round for me at ten-thirty, and there I was, settled down in the back, lighting a cigarette and watching the scenery slide past me. And not until that moment did it really hit me. I was going to see Hazel again. And I had no idea, absolutely none, why I was doing it.

I had enjoyed my time at Oxford. After all, when you've spent three years sitting on the deck of a destroyer, it's difficult not to enjoy a life as easy-going as that. It was irritating, in a way, to spend half of each year away from town, but it's only sixty miles – you can always get up to London for a show or a party, if you make the effort. Yes, all round it was very well worth it, especially as I met some people who've since proved very good friends, both in the business and outside it.

One thing it didn't do – and nobody was surprised – was to give me a thirst for book-learning. I'm a pretty well-informed person and like to know the score, but as far as I could see, the kind of information that comes under the heading of 'scholarship' was useless for any real purpose: all it did was clutter your brain. I went along with it, of course, sufficiently to pick up the magic letters after my name. They look nice on the firm's letterhead. And it had its interesting sides. But to be interested all the time, to give your days and nights to this stuff and never ask for anything better, you'd need a special kind of brain. And I knew only one man who had. Bill Gerard.

Bill lived for two things. His work, and Hazel. Where he got her I never knew. I mean, she was at the university, but how he came to nab her was a mystery to all of us. She was the goods. Tall, copper-headed, with a build on her that made your mouth water. And she was inseparable from Bill. You never saw her without him. All of us, at different times, tried to slide in and steer her away, but there was never anything doing.

Why the surprise? Lots of girls at that age attach themselves to a man and ask nothing better than to spend all their time with him. It makes them feel secure. There are women who can't bear freedom. It makes them feel lost, uncertain of their own identity from day to day.

Granted. But Hazel didn't look at all that type. There was a wildness about her. In her eyes, in the fullness of her mouth, in her face with a touch of the Mongol in its high cheekbones, there was something that looked out at you, and whatever that something may have been, it wasn't tameness or domesticity. So why did she stick to Bill, never showing any interest in anyone else, as the months lengthened into years?

The explanation we all gave at the time, whenever we discussed it behind their backs, was that Bill was going to marry Hazel. In our eyes that explained everything. Marriage, to us, was such a gigantic and unthinkable step, such a sacrifice in which the man gave up absolutely everything that made life worth living and only the girl benefited, that it seemed capable of resolving any puzzle. If Hazel already looked on Bill as her husband, well, naturally she was satisfied with him. I see now how shallow this explanation was. I know that the working of a girl's mind is more complex than that. Still, that was how we had it doped out, back in that first summer after the war.

Bill had been up at Oxford before the war and got through part of his course then, which was the reason why he took his finals a year ahead of most of us. I remember hearing him say once, in the Common Room, that he wanted to get over the undergraduate stage as soon as he could. It struck me as summing up in a few words the difference between him and the rest of us. Undergraduate life – a perfect excuse for taking it easy for a bit – suited the rest of us very well, but Bill wanted to take a header into the deep waters of 'research' and the rest of it that lay beyond. I had just enough imagination to be able to tell the kind of thing that went on in his mind. All the big adventures happened to him when he was sitting still. He had inward-looking eyes – even when he was looking into your face he was only seeing you mechanically, so to speak. His eyes took on the sparkle of real interest only when he was looking at a book, taking it down from the shelf and fingering it, leafing through the pages to see if it would interest him. And, of course, when he looked at Hazel. He was quite sure she interested him.

Well, I'd watched for my chance with the rest. And now, twenty years later, I was sitting back in my car, streaming down the highway, with lots of money in the bank and everything going very well, nice wife and kids, feeling as young as I ever did and certainly nothing like old enough to live in the past – and yet where I was going? To Bill's house, to see Hazel. Raising a ghost when I don't even believe in ghosts.

I don't myself use the expression 'in love', because it seems to me that that kind of biological need isn't love. Or, if it is, then I can claim to have been a great lover for years, in my single-minded devotion to grilled steak. Needs are needs, not ideals. Still, there are certain times and places in which it's very difficult not to fall into the kind of slushy idiom in which you speak of a yen for a girl as 'love', and Oxford in May and June is like that. If you've ever been there at that time, you won't need me to fill in the details. The young fresh grass, the blossoms and, over it all, that inciting river smell, all weed and minnows, that rises from the Thames and spreads over the whole town, suggesting lazy afternoons and indiscretions in punts. Add a few all-night college dances, with heavy flower scents coming through the dark summer nights, and everybody's well and truly launched. It all puts a young man into the state where if the right girl isn't there for him to project his 'love' fantasies on to, he'll go ahead and project them on to the wrong one.

Good fun? Brings a sentimental tear to the eye? Perhaps, if it works out right. For me, it didn't. I made the kind of mistake that's so difficult to understand when you look back on it at forty. I got steamed up over the wrong girl. Bill's girl. Oh, I tried to be sensible. I told myself that other girls had tawny eyes, and high cheekbones, and lithe, purposeful bodies. But it was no good – I wanted Hazel. And she was Bill's.

Having tried to be sensible and given that up, I tried the other thing. Full steam ahead and crash in. Worshipping from afar isn't my line. When I want things I go and get them, and at least if I don't get them I leave the marks of my teeth and nails for all to see. At first I tried to play it cool, waiting for the odd moment when Bill's back was turned and slipping in the casual invitation to come and drink a glass of sherry in my rooms. God knows, if she had turned up I'd have raped her and let the chips fall where they may. But it was always, 'Can I bring Bill?' and then, of course, I'd be landed with a situation I couldn't face, and would have to squirm out of it somehow.

Things went on like this until I heard from somewhere that they were going to get married straight away, as soon as Bill had got his degree. That stunned me. I remember the moment I first heard about it. My knees literally sagged and I felt I had to sit down. Of course I'd known they were booked to get married, but that was comfortably in the future. I'd never realized they were going to be about, in Oxford, as man and wife, so that I'd always be running into them. Because, as I learned at the same time, Bill was more or less certain to stay on. They were keeping a junior fellowship warm for him. So he'd be setting up house with Hazel, changing her name, branding her and leading her about as his own tame heifer right before my eyes. For a few hours I seriously considered leaving Oxford – going down there and then, at the end of my second year, and getting a job.

But my natural determination came back. I don't like having my plans interfered with. Not even the girl I was in 'love' with was going to have *that* kind of power over me.

All the same, I was in pretty considerable agony. I couldn't give my mind to enjoying life, so I tried to fill in the time by working, but of course I couldn't give my mind to that either. The days were flowing by without the slighest profit, a thing I can't abide: I'd had enough of that on the deck of that damned destroyer.

Then Fate, with its well-known sense of humour, gave me a throw of the dice. Just one throw.

It was a brutally hot day in the second week in June. I'd got up late after a sleepless night, and just about mustered the energy to get into my clothes and shamble out. It was somewhere between midday and one o'clock, and the paving stones were frying. I wasn't wearing a hat, and the sun fairly grilled the back of my neck as I walked slowly up the High. I couldn't decide whether to try and eat lunch, regarding it as breakfast, or step into a pub and start soaking up beer again. If I did, I knew I'd be too inert to snap out of it, so I'd probably drink till about three and then go back to bed, half drunk and with an empty stomach. Not an attractive thought. I was wondering in a bemused way, what I *was* going to do, and how much longer I could walk in this glaring heat without falling down in a fit of sunstroke, when I realized there was a female shape standing right in front of me and I was about to bump into it. Muttering an apology, I raised my eyes and found myself looking at Hazel.

'Oh,' I said. 'Er ... what are you doing here?' As if I'd met her in the Gobi Desert.

'Bill's taking a paper,' she said.

The heat crashed on my skull; my shirt was pasted to my back; and what with the fatigue, Hazel's nearness, and everything else, I was incapable of forming the simplest idea. Then it dawned on me. We were standing outside the Examination Schools. Bill was in there, scribbling away for dear life, unloading the knowledge that would bring him a degree, and the degree would bring him a job, and the job would bring him a marriage licence. . . .

'Come and have a drink,' I said, feebly groping for her arm.

'I'm waiting for Bill. He'll be out in a minute, and I'm going to cook him some lunch to save him having to sit in a stuffy restaurant in this heat.'

I looked at my watch. 'You're at least fifteen minutes too early,' I said. 'And after they finish, he'll be another five minutes getting out, which gives you twenty minutes to have a five-minute drink with an old admirer.' I leered at her, unleashing a cloud of breath that must have corroded the stonework of the Examination Schools, and at the same time wiped a boiling deposit of sweat off my neck. Prince Charming. And to cap it all, my eyes compulsively dropped to her magnificent bosom, and I knew I could have been arrested just for the thoughts that were going through my mind.

She demurred a bit more, but the cool bar was only a few steps away, and the pavement must have felt uncomfortably hot through her thin shoes. In a couple of minutes we were installed, I with a pint of beer and she a glass of chilled white wine. I looked at her, averted my eyes because of the pain of her beauty, took a gigantic swig of the beer, turned back to her, and all of a sudden it had happened. I was talking fast, blurting out the whole story of my need for her.

'Look, it's madness,' I said. 'A girl should never marry the first man she loves. What's going to happen when you grow up and change? No, listen to me for God's sake. There's just time. You're not married yet. I love you. I know I could make you happy. Look, we understand each other. You're not Bill's type. You're mine.'

'That's just it,' she said, slipping down from her stool. I reached out and for one shuddering instant my fingers closed round her smooth, shapely wrist. Then it struck me that she'd said something odd.

'What d'you mean. That's just it?' I said.

'I mean it's not a question of whose type I am,' she said. 'It's more a question of who I can trust. And trust myself with.'

'Come back!' I said loudly, as she made for the door.

'Easy, easy,' said the landlord. 'It's too hot for a disturbance.' He was trying to play it good-temperedly, but I could see from the hard look in his eyes that he was ready to throw me out. And Hazel had gone. All of a sudden I wanted to stop thinking about her. I drank the rest of my beer and ordered more. The landlord was mollified. We talked about cricket, and I got more voluble as pint after pint went down. But underneath it all I was aware that the meaning of Hazel's words was spreading across my mind like a stain over a tablecloth. She, the inwardly untamed, with the wild high cheekbones and the blood of a roamer in her veins, had chosen close-knit serious-eyed Bill. He was personable and attractive enough to take up her attention, and at the same time help her to keep herself reined in. She didn't trust herself, and she was damned right.

I slurred off a few more jokes to the landlord, and then lurched back to my flat and lay down on the bed. How I ever got up again I don't know. Everything felt broken inside me. Even at this distance of time, I'd rather not talk about it.

The next thing that stands out in my memory is being in the Common Room with one or two friends, drinking our way through a few bottles of very good sherry we'd got as a bargain. Term was over – in fact, it had been for about ten days – but we'd all stayed up a bit longer, because there was a series of dances and parties we didn't want to miss before everybody dispersed to London or abroad. Eight weeks wasn't enough for all the good times we tried to pack in an Oxford summer. I say 'we' because, though I was feeling utterly grim and blank inside, I went along with it. What can you do?

One thing you can't do is drink too much sherry at a time, and we were just thinking of corking up what remained and going out for a meal, when Bill came in. We were all pretty relaxed, so we hailed him jovially, though normally there was a fairly marked gulf between him and a roistering set like us, and poured him out a glass. His face was very set and white. At first I thought he was just tired, with the strain of doing all that work for his finals, but pretty soon the sherry warmed him up enough to start him talking, and it emerged that he was angry. Really fighting mad. Well, naturally we questioned him a bit: encouraged him to get it off his chest.

'This fellowship they're giving me,' he said in exactly the tone in which he'd have said, 'This wooden half-crown they gave me in my change.'

We hadn't known he had been given a fellowship, so a few vague noises of congratulation and we-knew-you-had-it-in-you rose into the air, and the bottle of Tio Pepe was poised for another libation.

'You don't understand,' he said, looking round hot-eyed. 'They've dug up some archaic college regulation and tied the whole thing to their own ungenerosity and lack of imagination.'

We looked blank.

'A condition of my election,' he said in a voice full of quiet fury, 'is that I reside. Live in.'

'Is that what's annoying you?' someone asked. 'What's wrong with having a free place to live and free dinners?'

'What's wrong with it is that I want to get married,' Bill said. 'I told them that, and they nodded indulgently, as if they were prepared to make allowances for a piece of adolescent folly. So I said it again, and this time they turned nasty. God! It was all so *predictable*!' He slammed his empty sherry glass down, almost hard enough to break it. 'I looked from one face to another, and there was no support anywhere. If they were married, they just avoided my eyes and pretended to be thinking about something else. And if they were rooted old bachelors, they looked at me with a kind of sneering triumph.'

At this point somebody interrupted with what purported to be a piece of gossip. Talk and laughter started up again, and the conversation was steered away from Bill's troubles. Everybody stood up, and started drifting to the door, sorting out jackets, hats, etc. But I couldn't leave it like that. I moved over to Bill and said, just for his ear, 'What's going to happen, then?'

'Happen?' he said, looking up at me as if he'd already forgotten talking to us.

'Are they going to stop you getting married?' I asked. I *had* to know.

'Listen,' he said, sitting up straight. 'Nothing is going to stop me marrying Hazel. If they can appeal to regulations, so can I. Academic celibacy has been dead for a century. They can force me to have a room in College, and they can force me to be there between midnight and eight in the morning – in term-time. That's the limit they can do.'

'But why don't they give in, if you're so determined?' I asked.

He shrugged. 'Every college has to have a statutory number of bachelor Fellows living within the walls.'

'To put the drunks to bed?' I suggested.

'That's about it. So of course they twist the arm of every young man they elect. Probably if they'd known I was going to get married they'd have passed me over for the job. But I'm damned if I'll give up my chosen career just because I've also chosen a wife.'

'That's right, teach the old crabs a lesson,' I said. Or something like that. And I hurried out, because suddenly I couldn't stand being with Bill any longer – couldn't stand looking at him or hearing his voice.

I spent most of the next three months in Amsterdam living it up like mad. I told my family I was at a reading party in a windmill, beside a quiet canal some miles out of the city. When I got home just a few days before it was time for the Oxford term to begin, they were concerned because I'd lost weight.

My eyes were positively popping out of my fleshless face, and I was as jumpy as a cat. They took me seriously to task for working too hard, so I solemnly promised I wouldn't do it any more. And off I went to Oxford for my last year, thankful at least that I'd filled in the time without too much moping over Hazel. But the energy I'd had to expend in keeping the thought of her at bay: the drink I'd had to consume, the night club proprietors I'd had to enrich, the women I'd had to chase! And at the end of it all, Hazel came bouncing back into my mind like something on the end of a rubber band. As soon as the train steamed in past the cemetery and came grinding into Oxford station, there she was in my brain, my blood, my bones, coming between me and everything else I wanted to enjoy. Only now I had to think of her as Mrs Bill Gerard.

Still, I kept up the heroic effort. For a whole month I packed my days and nights with meaningless things – meeting people, going to parties, even working. Sometimes, for stretches of eight or nine hours at a time, I forgot about Hazel altogether. I saw the pair of them in the street, now and then, but I always managed to duck down a side road and keep from having to confront them, and smile, and pass the time of day. And the Oxford summer which was still hanging about in odd wisps at the beginning of October, lost its magic and disappeared, and the crisp mornings and early evenings came in, making one feel brisk and businesslike. I was almost on the point of telling myself that the nonsense was out of my system, that I'd sweated it away and was cured.

And then, one pouring wet night in early December, it happened.

I was walking home from a party, wet through and in a king-size temper. I'd just been forced to get rid of my car; the proctors had withdrawn their permission to keep one in Oxford, owing to some fool misunderstanding with a policeman, and though I was tempted to chance it, just put it in a fresh garage and trust to chance that I'd never be stopped and though I was trust to chance that I'd never be stopped and questioned, I decided against crowding my luck. I didn't want them to start investigating me, or one or two things could easily have come to light which would have forced them to expel me, and I should have regarded that as a defeat on points.

So there I was, walking home through this soft, drenching rain. Midnight was beginning to chime out from various clocks – it would take about ten minutes for the whole lot to give their individual votes on the matter – and the party had broken up, because most of the guests were the law-abiding type who hadn't been able to beat the regulations and find themselves accommodation in places where they weren't persecuted with silly little rules, like having to be in at midnight. I had – which was one of the reasons why I didn't want the progs investigating me. But I was fed up: with rain, with the law-abiding little people, with the dreary party that had ended too soon.

The clocks bonged out, the rain splashed down, and the streets were empty except for a few hurrying figures. A city of the dead. I began to think longingly of a warm, dry bed, however lonely. Then I noticed two figures standing still, a little way ahead of me. I slowed down as I approached them: something about them told me they were people I knew.

Of course. And I stopped in my tracks. But why were Bill and Hazel standing by a wet wall, at midnight, talking in low voices? They were married: why weren't they at home in bed, or drinking cocoa by the last glowing embers?

Then I remembered Bill had to report at college every night at twelve, and stay there till eight before he could come home to breakfast. And they had been married about three months – the torture of it all! I saw the whole thing in a flash – how they would go to bed together at, say, nine o'clock; how, at eleven-thirty, just when that deep, contented sleep ought to have been setting in, Bill would have to get up, leaving Hazel there! He must have wanted that job very badly, I thought. Still, each to his taste. But why was she here with him? I stepped aside, into deep shadow. The splashing rain overlaid the sound of footsteps, and I knew they were unaware of me. I tried to hear what they were saying, but I wasn't quite near enough. Their attitudes told me they were arguing some point with a good deal of passion; she kept hanging on to his arm, and doing most of the talking; he was looking down at the ground, as if in mental conflict. Finally he looked up at her, and said something that was evidently meant to be decisive and was decisive, because she broke away from him, turned, and began to walk rapidly away. When she'd gone about ten yards, she stopped, and threw him just one glance, but it didn't alter his decision, and as I watched he took out a key, opened a door in the wall, and went in. The door closed, and suddenly there was nothing in the world except the rain falling in the street, the last chimes of midnight, the heavy wet stones of the wall, and Hazel's tall figure hurrying away.

I came out of my patch of shadow. I don't think any ideas had, at that stage, formed in my head. I was just drawn toward Hazel by the sheer pull of my desire for her. When she turned and looked back at Bill, I had seen her face. I can't describe it. I can only say that if she, or any girl with half her attractive power, had looked at me like that, with so much tenderness, so much need, and so much brave defiance that wasn't fooling anyone, I'd have dynamited the college rather than go through the door in the wall and shut it between us.

I quickened my pace so as not to lose her in the quiet streets we were approaching. I don't believe I had any thought except just to follow her until she got home, to keep my eyes on her until the last possible moment. You don't reason, or plan, at a time like that. I walked fast, fast, but even so I only just kept up with her swinging stride. She's magnificent, I found myself thinking. The words formed themselves over and over in my mind as if on a ticker-tape that had gone out of control: She's magnificent. She's magnificent.

Leaning forward into the rain, walking so fast I was almost running, I gained a little at a time until I was just behind her. I thought she must surely have heard my footsteps, but she never slackened her pace or turned round, and in my excitement I was almost breathing down her neck when suddenly she stopped at a garden gate, unlatched it quickly and swung it open. Then she saw me, there we were, facing each other with the gate between us.

Her face was wet, and for a moment I thought it was just the rain. Then I saw that her eyes were brimming. But her voice was quite steady when she spoke. 'What are you doing?' she asked me.

'Coming to see you.'

'You mustn't,' she said. 'Bill isn't here.'

'I know where Bill is,' I said.

Hazel made a small, tense movement that was half-way to a shrug. Then she turned and walked up the garden path, leaving me holding the gate. I went inside, shut it behind me and followed her.

She opened the front door, and I was right behind her. When it closed, the two of us were inside. She simply went on up the stairs as if I weren't there. They had the top flat.

Once we got inside she went straight into the bedroom and switched on the light. I followed. The gas fire was on, roaring away to itself. And there, in the centre of the room, was the bed Bill had climbed out of in the interests of his scholarly career.

Hazel stood for a few seconds, looking at me. Her eyes were still full of tears. I could feel the hard emptiness inside her. All that full bowl of love and emotion had been spilt on the ground, and there was, for a moment, nothing for anybody. Or anything for everybody, depending on how you cared to put it. Same thing, really.

My wet hair clung to my skull: my whole body was burning. Hazel looked at me with those tear-wet, empty eyes, as if I were a piece of furniture. And, in her world at that moment that's no doubt what I was. In fact, the next thing she did proved it. She turned away from me and began to undress, laying her clothes across a chair, exactly as if she were alone.

As for me, I just stood there. I knew what I was going to do, but beyond that I had no thoughts and no identity. I wasn't James Richards. I was just an event that was about to happen to Hazel.

Everything came off, and then Hazel walked straight past me to the light switch. *Click*. There we were, in the rosy half-dark. Then she padded over to the gas fire and put it out too. The red glow faded quickly. The dutiful wife, having walked with her husband as far as the little door in the college wall, had come back to their top-floor flat, turned off the light and the gas, and got into bed.

And if there was an uninvited presence there, too, was that her fault?

So much for my memories. But that was then and today was now. As we drove into the suburbs of Oxford, I began to feel horribly nervous, much more than I'd ever expected. All of a sudden I didn't want to see Bill, and even more strongly I didn't want to see Hazel. The car felt like a prison: it was so heavy, so smooth, so fate-like in the way it rolled along, carrying me towards Bill's house like a laboratory animal being shipped without malice to the place where it will be tormented. I hated the cool, impersonal neck and shoulders of Evans. The perfect chauffeur. All he did was drive the car, efficiently and without any feelings. He should have been a concentration camp *Kommandant*.

My tension rose towards a momentary peak, then sank back. My heart slowed down to a normal beat. Twenty years is twenty years. Hazel and Bill would be different people. And I? Oh, I was a different person. I had more money, for one thing, and that changes you. If you don't believe me, that's probably because you don't know anybody well who used to be poor and is now rich.

I got Evans to drop me at the end of their road, and told him to get lost and come back at six o'clock. That would give me time to get home for an eight o'clock dinner. The day was mapped out, controlled, safe. No matter what happened at Bill's, it would end at six o'clock, and a normal Sunday would close in again. Peace. I breathed easily as I found the house and went up to the front door.

A beaten-up garden with a swing. Kids. But the swing was old, and the grass under it wasn't worn away. So the youngest kid was too old to bother with the swing. I rang the bell.

A girl of about thirteen opened the door. She asked me if I were Mr Richards, and I said yes. All ready for me. No doubt the girl had listened to mealtime conversations in which Bill and Hazel talked about old times. James Richards? I can hardly recall his face. Was he a friend of yours? Not really – just up at the same time. Very true. I followed the girl into the living room and waited.

Not for long, though. One quick glance round the room – good, shabby furniture, lots of books, one high-quality reproduction and a dim daub that looked like an original – and all at once Hazel was coming in through the french windows, pulling off gardening gloves, and Bill was entering through the door, both at once. So I only had time to take one quick look at her before I turned to face him. All very confusing. What that first glimpse showed me was that time had thickened her figure but didn't seem to have made much difference to her face. It still had good skin and youthful outlines. She was holding a bunch of roses – must have been cutting them in the garden while waiting for me. The gardening gloves lent a delightfully informal touch. It was quite an entrance, though Bill spoilt it a bit by making his at the same time.

Bill seemed longer and thinner. His tightly massed hair had a tinge of grey. Apart from that, twenty years had done nothing to him, except deepen the lines of thoughtfulness that had already, when I knew him, begun to spread across his face. Or was that all? I looked at him again, more carefully, as he looked away from me at Hazel. Weren't his eyes different somehow? More inward-looking than ever? Gazing in not merely at his thoughts, but at something else, something he was keeping hidden or perhaps protecting.

Then we were chattering and taking glasses in our hands, and I came back to earth. For the first ten minutes we were all so defensive, so carefully probing, that nobody learnt anything. Bill had forgotten me altogether; that much was clear. He was engaged in getting to know me from scratch, very cautiously so as not to hit a wrong note, with the object of hitting me up for a big subscription to his African tomfoolery. I, for my part, was stonewalling and keeping my eyes open. I kept trying to absorb details about Hazel, but Bill was talking earnestly about African education, and the strain of appearing to concentrate while actually thinking about his wife proved so great that I decided it would be easier just to concentrate. So I did. I let him hammer away for about ten more minutes, and then the daughter, who seemed to be acting as parlourmaid, showed in another visitor. Evidently we were to be four at lunch.

The new arrival was called Paul something-or-other and

they all seemed to be on pretty cosy terms. Paul was a colleague of Bill's, also in the Plato-and-Aristotle business. But a very contrasting type. He was strongly built, with a bull neck and a domed forehead that looked like a battering-ram. It gave the impression of having a tremendous thickness of skull beneath it, so that I had a vision of him putting his head down and charging like a rhinoceros, and going straight through the wall of a house. His voice was a shock, though. It was weak and soft, not at all the voice that ought to be coming from that big chest. I decided he must have had some kind of disease that had affected his larynx.

'Is Bill telling you about Africa?' he asked me, sitting down comfortably with his glass in his hand. 'Don't tell me. It's a safe bet that he is.'

'I suppose I am a bore about it,' said Bill, looking eager and worried at the same time.

'Don't apologize,' this Paul said. 'We're dons, we're expected to be boring. We're not expected to be able to talk about anything but our own concerns when we meet visitors from the great world outside. Isn't that so?' he appealed to me.

'You said it, I didn't,' I fended him off. 'As it happens, Bill's African ideas don't bore me. I came down to hear him talk about them.'

'Well, don't let me stop you,' Paul said. He turned to Hazel and included her in his smile, which was bright and mechanical. 'I'm here for Hazel's cooking, but I promise not to interrupt.'

Did I imagine it? Or did some kind of signal, a brief flash too quick for the eye to follow, jump between the two of them? 'I'm here for Hazel's cooking.' Did my inner ear detect a layer of meaning, thin as onionskin, behind the words? Here for Hazel's what?

I turned back to Bill, and he began to chew my ear off again. Africa this, Africa that. After a while Hazel got up and went over to the sideboard to get more drinks. She collected our glasses, recharged them, brought them back, and also fidgeted about with little bowls of nuts and olives and so forth. As she moved about, against the steady background of Bill's voice, I watched her – not so much with my eyes, as with those antennae a man uses to keep contact with a woman who's moving about within a few feet of him. I felt, rather than saw, what she was doing – how she bent over, straightened, paused here and rustled rapidly there. And all of a sudden I had it. Don't tell me I'm wrong. I've never made a mistake yet.

She was playing around with this Paul.

How did I know? It's hard to put into words. Adultery has a kind of supersonic whine, too high for your ears to pick up unless you've done something to attune them. Well, I'd done a fair amount to attune mine. There was my past history with Hazel. Plus one or two other episodes in between. Nothing to do with this story, but I hear the note when it's sounded.

Bill had stopped talking for a moment. He was waiting for me to say something. And I had nothing to say, because it would have been hopeless to try and make him see how misguided all this African do-gooding was. I was going to have to keep my opinions to myself and even simulate a polite, constructive interest. That meant choosing my words with great care, or he'd be trying to tie me down to all sorts of definite obligations. And all the time I was conscious of Paul and Hazel, darting glances at each other over the rims of their drinks. At one point she handed him the dish of olives, and I watched like mad to see if he allowed his hand to brush against hers as he took one. That's usually the mark of people who are having an affair – the compulsion to touch each other. But he was clever, this Paul. It wasn't his first time. He looked just the kind of skilful cad that never gets caught.

And Hazel? What did she look like? I was trying to decide, and at the same time halting through a few sentences to keep Bill at arm's length, when fortunately there was a diversion. The thirteen-year-old girl came in, bringing a younger sister with her, aged about eleven. There was a certain amount of small talk, plus an argument about whether the son was expected to lunch or not. He was evidently the eldest, about nineteen and an undergraduate at his father's college. He was supposed to come home to lunch every Sunday, but he pleased himself and stayed away if it suited him. As they wrangled about whether he had or hadn't said he was coming, I was thinking about his age. Nineteen. Hazel must have conceived him in the very year when I last saw them. Perhaps – since all things are possible – it was even . . . I dismissed the thought at once.

They finally decided that the son wasn't coming, which relieved me considerably, and we all went in to lunch. Not having any domestic help, Hazel and the girls shared the job of fetching the food in from the kitchen and dishing it up. For a few minutes it was all coming and going, clattering dishes, arguing over where this was and where that was, while Bill and Paul and I stood waiting to take our seats at the table. It gave me a chance to take Paul in.

He was chatting to Bill with elaborate man-to-man casualness, a sort of old-colleagues-together tone under cover of which he was taking out some rather nasty ill nature. It was obvious that Bill irritated him considerably. I suppose a cuckold is always irritating, particularly so to the man who is putting him in that position.

'Of course, Bill's just marking time,' he said to me with a facetious grin that tried to rope me in on his side in the baiting game. 'Another three weeks and he'll be finished with Oxford. Already we're insubstantial – just wraiths, aren't we, Bill?'

'Are you really leaving as soon as that?' I asked.

'I shall be flying out,' he answered, 'to look round and see what kind of accommodation is available, and meet my African colleagues, and get some idea of the size of the job. I shan't be starting work, though, till late in September. So there'll be some time to fly back here and clear everything up at this end.'

'Clear everything up?' I said. 'You mean sell the house? Are you all going?'

Hazel was putting vegetable dishes on the table, and it seemed to me that she set them down hard, and rattled spoons and things unnecessarily, thrusting her presence into our midst as if she didn't want our conversation to go on. I saw too, a look of quick misery slide across Bill's face.

'We haven't quite decided yet,' he said.

'Will you carve, darling?' Hazel asked him in a brisk, over-riding voice. No talking about our family plans in front of strangers, was what she meant. I shot a look at Paul; he had his eyes discreetly lowered.

It's a mistake to be too careful; if you take pains not to let anything be seen anyone can tell you've got something you can't afford to show.

We chewed and swallowed, made meaningless conversation and watched each other. Hazel's eyes were bright. She seemed to me to be enjoying herself with an inner excitement that came glowing through her skin. Three men at once, even if one of them was only her husband. What was her game? How did she live her life now? I thought of those few minutes we had spent together, the blazing street and the shadowy bar.

'That's just it. It's a question of who I can trust myself with.' Her eyes had that same wild dimension inside them. What lay hidden in the twenty years since I had loved her?

As for Paul, I hated his plump hands. I hated him for her husband's sake, and for my sake, and for her own sake.

The situation was getting out of hand. I longed for six o'clock, but it was only a quarter to two. More than four hours of this! A sense of reckless power came over me. I no longer cared what I did; I only wanted to leave some kind of mark on the situation, something that would make them remember the day I visited them. 'James was here. He broke this, and this, and that over there.'

Paul was needling Bill again. Some rigmarole about teaching philosophy in a hot climate.

'Passions run high,' he was saying. 'Remember Pascal, where he says he only believes histories related by people who are ready to let themselves be torn to pieces?'

'What kind of bunk is that?' I asked him. I could hear my voice being rough and challenging, like one street corner lout working up a quarrel with another.

'It's in the *Pensées*,' he said, giving me a contemptuous glance.

'Very uncharacteristic, though,' Bill intervened, trying to preserve good humour. 'Besides, Pascal's attitude to history wasn't the same as his attitude to philosophy.'

'Look, I don't know anything about Pascal and I don't want

to know,' I snarled. 'But I can see when somebody's talking in a damned silly irresponsible way.'

Bill looked at me wide-eyed, conveying shock and reproof, but I didn't care. I wanted to tread on this Paul with his soft, mocking voice and his thick neck. I was never going to see any of them again, so what did it matter? If I can't give you any money for your Africans, Bill, I thought, I can at least insult the man who's battening on your sexual life. Thrusting in between you, and Hazel, and my ghost.

'You certainly believe in plain speaking, don't you?' Paul said, leaning forward and looking at me with aggression in his eyes and mouth.

'I believe in ordinary common decency,' I said. 'If I couldn't stop myself from mocking at a man's ideals, I wouldn't come and eat at his table.'

At this, Hazel got up abruptly, pushed her chair back with a loud scrape, and left the room, beckoning the daughters with her. And they went out too. It was her way, I suppose, of trying to bulldoze the quarrel to a standstill before it went any further. But I wasn't going to let go until I had taught our fine friend a lesson.

'Nobody's mocking any ideals,' he came back at me in his reedy voice. 'It's just that you're out of touch with the academic idiom. Irony always is misunderstood by . . .' he shrugged.

'By peasants like me?' I said. 'All right, don't spare me your Oxford complacency.'

'Please, both of you,' Bill said helplessly. We turned and looked at him, but all he could say was, 'Please,' again.

'Don't interrupt us, Bill,' I said. 'We're quarrelling.'

'I don't know why,' he said. 'It's a bit hard on me, as your host – '

'I'm finding it rather interesting, to tell you the truth,' said Paul. 'I have so little contact with the great world of business and practical affairs.' He brought out the words with a thick fat sneer. 'After spending my whole adult life in an atmosphere of free discussion, with give-and-take among everybody, I'd forgotten how tycoons exercise their power – tongue-lashing and bullying anyone whose tone they don't like.'

'You've got me wrong,' I told him seriously. 'Any decent

person would react like me, tycoon or not. If you've spent your life among people who never defend their friends when they're insulted, you may call that equality and give-and-take, but I call it spinelessness.'

He was pale with anger, but the old ironic detachment didn't slip for a moment. 'That's how the exercise of intelligence always does strike the outsider,' he came back. 'You think I'm insulting Bill because I make jokes with a sceptical tinge about his – '

'That's right. It's the tinge I don't like. I don't go by your rule book, that says a tinge is only to be answered by another tinge, till the whole thing dies away in a kind of sunset of tinges.' I was surprised at how well, and how much, I was talking. Adrenalin had stimulated me. 'I don't think you should accept Bill's hospitality if the only thing you contribute is a permanent cold sneer.'

Paul got up and said. 'I'll go now, Bill. There's no point in prolonging this. Your friend doesn't like me, and the situation could only develop in a way I'd be sorry for.'

I said, 'If that's a veiled threat to punch me in the face, come outside and try it.'

'James! For God's sake!' said Bill sharply. 'What's come over you?'

I could see he was puzzled, sad, angry, and very much regretting that he'd ever asked me to his house. So after Paul had walked out, which he did silently and quickly, I made him a little speech.

'Look, Bill,' I said. 'I've been guilty of a loss of self-control – I admit it and I apologize for it. I didn't like Paul; and in particular I didn't like the way he seemed to be laughing behind his hand at you and your ideas. All right, tell me I don't understand Oxford ways, tell me I'm coarse and imperceptive. But don't let it spoil our day. I haven't seen you for all these years, and I'm here to learn all about your plans and hopes over this African business. When I've gone, you can go and see Paul and make excuses if you like. Tell him you didn't know I'd degenerated into such a brute. Tell him anything. Only let's go and sit in the garden, in the sun, and talk about Africa.'

Just at that moment, Hazel came back in. She was looking

proud and challenging; not angry, exactly, but very ready to face anybody down.

'Paul's gone, I see,' she said.

'Don't wrap it up, Hazel,' I said. 'I insulted Paul and picked a quarrel with him, and that's why he left. I've just been mollifying Bill – at least,' I said, turning to him, 'I hope I have.'

Bill smiled to show that he accepted my conciliatory efforts, but Hazel looked at me stonily and said, 'All right, I won't wrap it up. Why did you do it?'

'I didn't like his attitude to Bill.'

'How do you know what his attitude to Bill is?'

Instead of answering, I threw her a searching look. She was standing behind Bill, where he couldn't see her face, and for an instant she looked me right in the eyes with a most curious expression. Half provocative and half conspiratorial. Very much as if to say, 'Go ahead, quarrel with me, interfere with my private concerns, and we'll see who comes off best – I'll probably enjoy it.'

Bill and I went outside, and in the excitement of telling me all about Africa he soon forgot the fracas with Paul.

Bill had the gift of being able to concentrate on a topic, pour his energies into it, and at the same time blot out all annoyances and problems on the fringe of his life. I admire that gift. It's probably the one indispensable condition for getting anything done. Because whose life isn't in a mess? In one way or another?

And certainly Bill's was. I watched him, and sized the situation up, as he droned on. There was a flushed eagerness in his face when he talked about his work in Africa, a kind of nervous enthusiasm that doesn't suit a man of forty-odd. Come to that, he wouldn't have had it in the days when I'd known him before. He was more self-contained then. This excitement was stirred up by some inner need. And I knew what need. He was running away from Oxford, from the life he had lived there for twenty years. And that meant only one thing. Hazel had somehow managed to kill his love for her. He was channelling everything into his idealistic harebrained scheme because it offered an escape from her. He had been hurt badly, and he was wild to get away before she hurt him any more.

As I reached this conclusion, Hazel was at my side with a tray. Tea in the garden. All very idyllic. And I noticed once again that she grouped herself outside Bill's field of vision.

'Are you looking forward to Africa, Hazel?' I asked stirring tea.

She looked up quizzically, as if I couldn't really be as stupid as the question made me sound, and Bill answered for her.

'I'm afraid it's all in the balance still. I mean, Hazel's never been to Africa, and before we take the step of transferring the whole household there, she's going to come and look round for a bit.'

'There are the children to think of,' Hazel added, but I didn't have to be very clever to understand she wasn't bothering about the children so much as looking forward to getting Bill away for a few years, while she was still young enough to cut a swath among the Pauls of this world.

So to test her I said, 'It'll be lonely for you, living in this house by yourself, if you don't go with Bill.'

'Oh, I can fly home for a goodish part of each vacation,' Bill put in. As he spoke I was watching Hazel. She shot him a sidelong glance that told me all I wanted to know, then looked up at me.

'I expect I'll manage,' she said. 'Somehow.'

After that, I had the whole picture. Bill and I sat back in our deck-chairs for another round of African facts and figures, and I fobbed him off every time he brought the subject round to the amount he could expect from my firm. The son came lounging round the side of the house – he looked sufficiently like Bill to advertise a no-accident conception, but apart from that he was just a typical modern undergraduate, narrow jeans, wide haircut and dirt. We were introduced, and he slouched off again. Then, somehow, it was nearly six, and I was getting ready to go. I knew Evans would have the car gliding to a standstill outside the gate at precisely eighteen hundred hours. I had to go, that was all there was to it, and my curiosity about Bill and Hazel would just have to feed on what I'd managed to pick up. All I knew was that it had gone wrong. Marriage to him hadn't done what she had counted on it to do for her. It hadn't held her steady. She'd gone wild at some stage and stayed wild.

But what stage? Early or late? Who had first cut the rope that held her to him?

'Well, I must get ready to go,' I said to Bill. I heaped the usual thanks and compliments, and looked round for my hat. He called Hazel out, and the two of them stood looking at me.

'I'll write to you,' I said to Bill, 'as soon as I've had a chance to discuss this with my fellow directors.'

I hoped the insincerity in my voice wasn't coming through as strongly to him as it was to me.

Then the eleven-year-old came to the french window and said my car was here. I held out my hand to Bill. Good-bye to the whole thing. One more unsolved mystery, anchored to a memory. But Hazel was saying something.

'I've got to call in and see Moira Davidson (or some such name). Perhaps James wouldn't mind dropping me off. It's not far from Carfax.'

James didn't have any choice in the matter. In a couple of minutes we were driving off, all by ourselves in a big cushiony car. I've always refused to have one of those cars with a glass panel isolating the driver, but now I regretted it.

'Why did you come, James?' she asked me, straight away, as soon as we started moving.

'To see you,' I said.

'Why? Just curiosity?'

I nodded. 'If that's what you want me to say. I'll say it.'

She made an impatient gesture. 'Don't be *cautious*. I won't have it.'

'Well,' I said, 'I'm not going to be *in*cautious. We're not alone, for one thing.' I kept my voice down and hoped Evans's hearing wasn't as sharp as I was afraid it probably was.

She leaned back and looked away from me as she said. 'You didn't like Paul, did you?'

'Not much.'

'Could you say why?'

'I was jealous,' I said.

She turned and looked at me now, 'You could see, then?'

'Anybody could.'

'Bill doesn't,' she said quickly.

The car halted at a red light, throbbed, started again.

'I expect Bill would rather not see,' I said. 'But it isn't any business of mine.'

We went round a corner, and her body swayed against mine. To steady herself, she put her hand on my knee. And to unsteady me, she left it there for a moment or two longer. Before she took it away she lifted those big, tawny eyes to mine, and I saw that they were still the eyes of a girl.

'It is, James,' she said.

'It is what?'

'Business of yours.'

What was she telling me? That I'd knocked a hole in the sea-wall, and after that the waters had gone on flooding in from that day to this? Was I the assassin of Bill's happiness?

'When did it go wrong, Hazel?' I asked. 'Between you and Bill?'

She looked at me steadily. 'You were there,' she said.

I wiped sweat off my face. A man doesn't like to feel that his innocent pleasures have given somebody twenty years of trouble, with at least twenty more in store. Bill was right: Africa was the answer.

'Well, here's where I'm going,' she said, pointing to a side street we were approaching. I leaned forward and asked Evans to stop.

'The end of the road will do,' she said. 'I'll walk down.'

The car slid to a halt, and Evans got out to open the door for Hazel. I calculated we had five seconds in which he would be out of earshot. 'Listen, Hazel,' I said. 'When Bill goes to Africa, you know where to find me.' I felt hot and reckless. After all these years I was as fast in the situation as ever.

'I'll be closing this place up,' she said, 'and getting a flat in town. The girls will be away from home, anyway.'

So that was fixed. Then Evans opened the door.

'Well, good-bye,' I said.

She smiled in at me briefly, straightened her back and walked off to her phoney social call, without looking behind.

What happened next? Nothing yet. It's still to come. All that was six months ago, and the other day I had a note from Hazel giving me her London address. I'll be looking her up. I mean, I'm married, but not as married as all that. But first, I sent Bill a fat contribution to his African fund. I mean a really fat one that I had to bulldoze through against the resistance of everyone else in the firm. It's enough to underwrite a whole department of his scheme, and in fact he's written back to say that he's putting my name to it. The James Richards Scholarship.

I feel rather good about that, on the whole. I mean, I realize that to teach these blacks a lot of elaborate skills is pure economic hara-kiri. But then hara-kiri is a very dignified business. And it pleases me to think that, in her own way, Hazel has been a help to Bill in his work. After all, that's how it should be.

Down Our Way

'God made us all different. Don't talk back to your mother,' said Mr Robinson.

'It's not the blacks I mind. They don't know any better,' said Mrs Robinson. 'But a man like that, knocking on people's doors and making trouble. There ought to be a law against it.'

'I expect there is, come to think of it,' said Mr Robinson. 'Appearing in disguise on the public highway.'

'Not now,' said Arthur Robinson, blowing on his tea. 'In olden days, yes. But it wouldn't work today. What with all these wigs and that, and not being able to tell whether it's a girl or a boy till you come right up to 'em – ' he expelled a harsh blast of air that sent his tea climbing dangerously high up its white glazed wall. 'You'd have to put half the country in prison.'

'Good job too,' said Mrs Robinson. She cut her piece of fruit-cake into sections, vigorously. 'They want teaching a good lesson, some of 'em. Dirty little madams.'

'The black fellers have got to live, mum,' said Doris Robinson with her usual stolid defiance.

'Nobody's stopping them,' said Mr Robinson. 'They're welcome to live as long as they stay where the good Lord put 'em. But they shouldn't come pouring into a white man's country. That's what I say and I've got the Bible to prove it.'

'Some people don't reckon the Bible proves anything,' said Doris. 'After you, Arthur. I like jam, too.'

'They ought to be ashamed, then,' said Mrs Robinson. 'Dirty colour-blind little madams. They don't care who they're with, so long as it's a man.'

'Well, they've got a point,' said Doris, attacking the jam.

'Make allowances, mum,' said Arthur. 'I expect that's what

it feels like when you're twenty-six and haven't got a husband yet.'

'Why don't you go and give all your blood to the Red Cross?' queried his sister indifferently.

'I bet you'd go out with a darkie fast enough,' said Arthur, disappointed at Doris's calm.

'I would if I liked him.'

'You want to read your Bible, my girl,' said Mr Robinson, getting up from his chair with slow dignity and going to look for his pipe. 'The sons of Ram shall bruise thy heel, and thou shalt bruise his head. Remember that.'

'Rough play in the Second Division,' said Arthur.

'The blacks can't help it,' said Mrs Robinson with a look of determined fair-mindedness. 'It's a man like that I'd put in prison. Blacking his face and knocking on people's doors.'

'They'll do anything to get a story,' said Arthur. 'I saw a play about it on the telly. They have to make something happen, else there's nothing to put in the paper.'

'They want to mind their own business,' said Mr Robinson through a cloud of pipe-smoke. 'They'd have plenty to put in the paper if they'd read their Bible.'

'Well, it's this neighbourhood,' said Doris. 'That's what everybody was saying at work today. He's working his way round East London and we can expect him here any time.'

'He won't have any trouble with the birds if he comes round this way,' said Arthur. 'Soon as they see a darkie they start running. Towards him.'

'Jealousy, that's your trouble,' said Doris. 'No wonder you can't keep a girl-friend, with them pimples.'

'If they weren't a lot of ignorant little madams,' said Mrs Robinson, 'they'd sooner have a nice clean English boy than a blackie, even with a few pimples.'

'Let's shut up about pimples shall we?' said Arthur. 'I'm having my tea.'

'You know what it'll say in the paper next morning, when he knocks on the door and you turn him away,' said Doris. 'Mr and Mrs Fred Robinson, who've been advertising in their front window with a room to let for the last six months, turned away the very first person that asked about it because he was coloured.'

'Who cares what it says in the paper?' Mr Robinson demanded. 'An Englishman's home is his castle.'

'Does it say that in the Bible?' asked Doris innocently.

'You watch your tongue, Doris,' said Mrs Robinson. 'That's all I say to you, watch your tongue.'

There was a knock at the street door.

'If that's him,' said Mr Robinson, 'tell him to go home and wash the black off his face.'

'And not come making trouble, just to get a story,' Arthur added righteously.

Doris was moving her chair back from the table when she saw that her mother had risen and was going into the passage.

'Be careful what you do, Mum,' she called.

'I know what I'm about,' said Mrs Robinson shortly.

All three listened intently as the door opened and Mrs Robinson's voice came to them down the hallway. But they could make out nothing except an occasional broken phrase, 'Don't think so,' 'I'll tell him,' 'shouldn't expect.' The other voice was a man's, but they caught nothing it said.

After a few minutes Mrs Robinson closed the front door and came back to them.

'Was that him?' Arthur asked.

'No. Mr Prothero,' she replied.

'Mr who?'

'The young man from the church. The curate. Mr Venables had sent him round.'

'And why didn't Mr Venables come his high and mighty self?' demanded Mr Robinson from beside the fire. 'After eight years as sidesman, I'm not worth his while to drop in on his way past?'

'That's what he wanted to talk about,' said Mrs Robinson. 'Said Mr Venables was sorry to hear you was giving it up.'

'You told him why, didn't you?'

'Yes. He wanted to come in and talk to you, but I said I couldn't have you bothered. Said the doctor told you to keep out of draughts with your legs. And I asked him straight out, could he deny that the church was draughty?'

'Specially round the sides, where I had to walk,' said Mr

Robinson. 'Eight years I took my legs down the draughtiest part of that church. Enough's enough, I say.'

'I never can understand that,' said Arthur reflectively. 'The church business. The same service going on in hundreds of churches at the same time. Wasting manpower like that, how stupid can you get? They should have one central service and televise it.'

'Tune in to channel fourteen and go on your knees on the hearthrug,' said Doris satirically.

'Well, there's more sense to that than what they do,' said Arthur. 'If Dad'd knelt on the hearthrug for thirty years instead of in cold draughty churches, his legs'd be as good as mine now.'

'Yours'll never come to any harm through bending your knees, that I will say,' Mr Robinson remarked.

'Never mind all that,' said Mrs Robinson, who had been thinking. 'This man. If he comes, I've decided what to do.'

'You'd better take the notice down, till the whole thing's over,' said Mr Robinson.

'No. That'd be running away. I've got a better idea. Welcome him.'

'*Welcome* –' Arthur was beginning in astonishment.

'Pretend to take him for a real darkie. After all, it's only by chance that we know about it. Nothing's been in the paper yet. I'll pretend not to suspect anything, be as nice as pie. That'll take the wind right out of his sails, make him drop the whole silly idea.'

'Ask him for a week's rent in advance. He'll have plenty of expense money,' said Mr Robinson.

Doris began to clear away the dishes. 'I think it's childish, if you ask me,' she said into the air.

'Childish?' said her mother. 'Who started it? What's more childish than blacking your face and knocking on people's doors?'

There was another knock, and she hurried down the passage; it was the next-door neighbour, wanting to borrow a cookery book. A few minutes later she ran to the door again, and made short work of a salesman proffering details of an encyclopedia. The atmosphere of expectancy began to leak away; Mr Robinson, dozing over the evening paper, had almost dismissed the matter from his mind.

But after half an hour the summons again. Mrs Robinson grumbled her way to the front door without haste, but this time she was longer in coming back, and the family were roused into sudden attentiveness by the bright, welcoming tones of her voice, which now reached them clearly.

'This way, will you please? I'd like you to meet Mr Robinson and our son and daughter ... we're all at home ... This is the front room, we've just cleared away our tea ... This way.' She entered looking over her shoulder at someone who was following her, and making little mincing movements of her head and body that made her look like a clumsily operated puppet.

Mr Robinson, Arthur and Doris all turned their eyes expectantly towards the doorway. At once, they were rewarded with a sight that froze them rigid with sheer surprise and, in the case of Arthur, with fury.

The newcomer was a stocky, broad-faced West Indian wearing a startlingly white raincoat and carrying a shiny plastic cap in his hand. The raincoat, as perhaps it was meant to do, concealed the clothes he was wearing under it, except for the bottom of his trousers, which appeared to be fairly voluminous at calf-level and caught in sharply at the ankles. His shoes were cracked, but clean and polished. As he came through the door, he looked cautiously from face to face and said, 'Good evening to all.'

'It's lucky the family are all at home,' said Mrs Robinson brightly. 'Then we can all get acquainted at once. This is Arthur, this is Doris, and this our Dad, Mr Robinson. They're all out at work all day and the young ones seem to be out most of the nights as well, but you know what young people are these days. Of course it's up to you whether you go out in the evenings or stay in your room – you're quite free to suit yourself entirely.'

'Thank you, missis,' said the man. His brown face split in a gleaming smile. 'Can I see the room now?'

'I'll take you up,' said Mrs Robinson. 'It's a nice quiet room with a bay window on the street. This is a very quiet street, I expect you've noticed. Never a bit of noise from traffic or the neighbours. Of course it's a very quiet neighbourhood. I *have* been told as I ought to charge ten shillings a week extra for the quiet, as an amenity, sort of thing, but I don't. What I say is, if we have the luck to live in a nice quiet street, we'll share our good fortune with other people. Excuse me, I'll lead the way.'

She went out and up the stairs, followed by the stranger. Hardly had the man's broad back vanished through the doorway, when Arthur let out a prolonged whistle of astonishment.

'Phe-e-e-e-ew!' He mopped his brow. 'She really thinks it's him.'

'She can't do,' said his sister.

'She *must* do. That's why she's sweet-talking him. Wants him to go away and write in the paper what a nice welcome he found at 46, Crescent Street. She's mad! She's mad! What'll she do when she finds out?'

'Well,' said Mr Robinson, retiring behind the paper, 'she'll have to do something. I want no part of this. She got him in and she'll get him out.'

Footsteps bumped down the stairs.

'I'm glad to say,' Mrs Robinson beamed, 'that Mr – er – '

'Major. Samuel Henry Major.'

'That Mr Major likes the room and he's going to take it. When would you like to come in, Mr Major?'

'Tomorrow, please, missis. I'll bring my cases over in the afternoon. I've got one more night to go in the place I'm staying now. I've paid up to the Wednesday and I don't want to give him a golden handshake.' Again the grin flashed out.

Mrs Robinson, standing behind Mr Major, threw a triumphant glance at her family. Her dignified face did not lend itself to anything as playful as winking; nevertheless, it conveyed the suggestion of a wink. 'Look at me leading him up the garden path!' her expression said.

Two ferocious scowls (male) and one look of pure pity (female) flashed back at her. The whole exchange took approximately one second.

'I've told Mr Major our terms,' Mrs Robinson went on. 'Three pounds a week or three pounds fifteen with light housekeeping.'

'Mr Robinson snatched the pipe out of his mouth and said quickly, 'But when we discussed it you said – '

'Never mind,' Mrs Robinson interrupted him with equal haste. 'I like to keep our charges reasonable. What I say is, we've had good luck – let's share it with others.' And once again she gave that quick glance of complicity.

Mr Robinson, defeated, took up the paper again. This left Arthur as the only defender of the citadel. He stared insolently at Mr Major. 'Are you taking the room just for yourself? Or bringing anybody else in?'

'My family are back home,' said Mr Major. 'In Trinidad,' he explained. 'Here is their photograph. Three boys and a girl. My wife will bring them when I save the money, like.' He took a photograph from his wallet and held it out to Arthur, who frowned and kept his arms by his sides. After a moment Doris took the photograph from Mr Major's hand and looked at it.

'What a nice family,' she said, 'I expect they miss you.'

'Photographs!' said Mrs Robinson's expression. 'The lengths these newspapers will go to!'

'I miss *them* every day,' said Mr Major simply. 'That's why I'm glad to get a room so reasonable. I'm saving every shilling I get. The fare is a lot of money. But,' he smiled, 'I'll make it.'

'This the first place you've tried?' Arthur had not taken his hard stare from Mr Major's face.

'No. I tried several before,' said Mr Major briefly.

'Wouldn't have you, I suppose?' Arthur pursued.

'They were full up,' said Mr Major. His face was without expression.

A silence filled the room. Mrs Robinson seemed to be debating inwardly whether to throw down the gauntlet and tell the man she knew he was a reporter and not a West Indian at all. Perhaps to avert the hideous farce this would involve, Doris asked nervously, 'Do you find it lonely over here?'

'Why, you got any suggestions?' said Arthur in a savage undertone.

'I go to the Social Club a lot,' said Mr Major, ignoring Arthur's question or not hearing it. 'I have lots of friends down there. Corner of Hubbard Street and Acacia Street. They get a very nice type. No need to spend money. I just drink a cup of tea and I stay and chat with my friends. I tell them, when my family comes over I'll give up tea for a while and celebrate with them.'

There was another silence, and Mr Major finally said, 'I'll be off down there now. Thank you very much, missis. I'll bring my cases along tomorrow night.'

'Where d'you work?' Mr Robinson suddenly asked, as if to pin down a vital piece of information before it was too late.

'On the electric,' said Mr Major. Evidently feeling this reply to be sufficiently meaningful, he smiled again, said 'Good night to all,' and retreated along the hall-way, his shoulder brushing the wall as he went past the umbrella stand.

The door closed behind him, and the Robinsons were left in an unnatural silence and stillness: the entire family seemed to have shrunk to four pairs of eyes, three accusing and one defensive.

'All right, go on, Mother,' said Mr Robinson at last. 'Tell us how you're going to get out of this one.'

'What is there to get out of?' Mrs Robinson asked stonily, but with a curious deadness in her voice which indicated that she was playing for time.

'You know good and well what there is to get out of!' Arthur's voice came out high-pitched and unsteady. 'You've gone and let the room to a real nigger. You thought you'd be clever and take a rise out of the man, and you've ended up with a nigger in the house along with your own family.'

Doris got up abruptly. 'I'm off out,' she said. 'I'll leave you clever ones to sort it out among yourselves. P'raps Dad can find the answer in the Bible.'

'You leave the Bible out of this, my girl,' said Mr Robinson severely. 'There's no call to be blasphemous – bringing the Bible in where it's no call to be.'

'How are you so sure that isn't the man with his face blacked?' Mrs Robinson persisted feebly.

'Oh, get your glasses changed, Mum,' Arthur snapped. His forehead was red with the enormous anger inside him. 'If you can look at a face like his and still think the colour'd *wash off*, you must be more stupid than you look.'

'Don't talk to me like that,' his mother rallied, glad to have some familiar ground to stand on. 'Stupid, is it? You'd all be in a right mess without me, even if I am stupid. Sometimes I think I'll walk out and see how you all get on, you – '

'Don't let's get on the argy-bargy,' said Mr Robinson, raising his hand like a traffic policeman. 'Arthur, don't talk like that to your mother. And you, Mother, don't take any notice of him. He's overstrained. What we want to know is, how are we going to get out of this mess?'

'That's right,' said Arthur fiercely. 'Mess is right. The first darkie to come knocking at the door and we take him straight in. Beat that for a mess.'

Doris, who had been upstairs to change her dress, came down and poked her head in at the door of the living-room.

'Well?' she said brightly. 'Figured your way out of it yet?'

'Don't worry,' said Mrs Robinson with dignity, 'I'll take another look at him when he comes back, and if it's true that I've made a mistake – I say if it's true – I'll soon get rid of him.'

'How?' Doris asked. Her voice lost its lightness and she drew her brows together. 'What d'you mean?'

'You don't think I'm really going to have a darkie in my house?' asked Mrs Robinson simply.

Doris looked for a long moment at her mother's impassive face. Then, silent, she turned and went down the hallway. The front door banged.

'What's the scheme, then, Mum?' asked Arthur. He felt in his jacket pocket for cigarettes, and looked across at her hopefully.

'When he comes back,' said Mrs Robinson, 'I shall just tell him there's been a mistake and he can't have the room after all.'

'A mistake?' Arthur was disappointed. 'What kind of a mistake would that be, then? How can it be all right for him to have the room one evening, and not all right the next? You'll have to do better than that.'

'Yes, Mother,' Mr Robinson umpired from his armchair, 'you'll have to give him a reason.'

'Reason?' said Mrs Robinson massively, 'reason? whose house is it?'

'You've offered a room to let,' said Mr Robinson, 'a man's

taken it, and even if he is a blackie you can't just tell him you've changed your mind.'

'Think what the papers'd print about *that*,' said Arthur. He'd go straight and sell 'em the story for fifty quid. They know where the money is.'

'All right,' said Mrs Robinson placidly. 'P'raps we'll have to have him in the place for a day or two. But it won't be long. He'll soon put a foot wrong and as soon as he does I'll have him out.'

'Put a foot wrong?' Arthur queried. 'Like how?'

'Like anything at all,' said Mrs Robinson. 'The lodger never lived who didn't leave the bathroom dirty, or smoke in bed or make a noise taking his boots off at night, or have undesirables in his room. If you take a lodger, you have to make all sorts of allowances or else you'd be asking him to move out within three days. Well, this one'll be on his way quicker than that.' She gave a short, scornful laugh. 'I haven't lived fifty years to end up not being mistress in my own house.'

Arthur, contented, lit his cigarette and began to fiddle with the television set. Mr Robinson, holding the evening paper on his knee, looked over at his wife's face. For the first time in twenty years, he looked at Mrs Robinson and really saw her. Then, slowly, his eyes dropped and he went on reading the paper.

Goodnight, Old Daisy

'I've told you before, you're welcome to stay at home, Father,' said Mrs Foster. Her voice was righteous but with an undertone of exasperation. 'If you want to spend your days hanging about in that draughty place, you've only yourself to blame.'

'Blame for what?' Mr Greeley asked mildly. He was moving slowly towards the front door, buttoning up his macintosh: his cap and muffler were already on.

'If you catch your death, of course,' said Mrs Foster. 'You've got a warm, comfortable home here, and goodness knows it costs me and Cyril enough trouble and money to keep it up. You could sit by the fire and read the paper, and no one to disturb you, as long as the children are at school, and they stay to dinner now.' She swept her duster in a wide arc across the already dust-free sideboard. 'And you have to go out every blessed day, down to that draughty place. If you lived in the workhouse I could understand it.'

Mr Greeley paused, deeply considering her words.

'It was my life, Nora,' he said at last. 'I don't go down there to annoy you. But I don't want to sit by the fire all the time. I like to go and see the old girl. It was my life, remember.'

'Well, I won't hinder you if that's your idea of enjoying yourself,' said Mrs Foster. I've told you you're welcome to stop at home. At least it's warm here, and with the cost of heating what it is that's *something*, I should think. Even if you don't appreciate it.'

Mr Greeley turned his weak old eyes on his daughter and faced her with a faded dignity that recalled the fine man he had once been, though not to Mrs Foster, who did not remember a time when she had not considered him old and worn-out.

'We've had this before, Nora,' he said. 'If I like to go down and look at the old girl, well, that's not to say I don't regard the kindness you show me in giving me a home, you and Cyril.'

'When you catch your death, you'll come to me to be nursed,' she said, polishing. 'They don't keep that place warm enough.'

'I've never coddled myself,' said Mr Greeley. 'If I should fall ill, send me to a hospital. You won't never have to nurse me.'

Straightening his shoulders, he marched defiantly to the door and out. The tension produced by his daughter's nagging had caused his heart to beat fast, sending his thin blood coursing quickly through its channels, but this did little enough to warm him against the icy wind that blew round the unsheltered bus-stop. He drew his macintosh tightly round him; much worn and threadbare, it was better than nothing, and he could not afford to buy himself a new coat and would not ask his daughter for the money.

While Mr Greeley waited, several other people gathered at the bus-stop, and one of them, a woman in her thirties, greeted him.

'Going into town, Mr Greeley?'

'Just to the Collection,' he replied. 'I generally go down and have a look at the old girl.'

Furred and scarved against the wind, she looked at him uncomprehendingly. Nora's old dad. She'd seen him in the background when she and Don went round for an evening. Nice of Cyril to put up with him really, and him pretty near ga-ga. The Collection? What did he mean?

'That's right,' she said vaguely, her gaze travelling past the old man in search of something interesting enough to hold her attention.

The bus, coming into view, spared her any further social effort. When it halted, the knot of waiters, elevated now to the dignity of passengers, climbed thankfully into its warm interior.

'The Collection, return,' said Mr Greeley to the conductor.

The railway museum was officially known as the Phipps Historical Railway Collection, in honour of some long-dead director who had given funds to start it, and Mr Greeley considered it beneath the Collection's dignity to be known as anything else. Some of the bus conductors knew what he meant, others did not; but by persevering he hoped, in time, to instruct them all.

This morning the conductor, a youth of about twenty, seemed not to hear Mr Greeley. He took the fares from two other passengers and then returned with, 'Where to, dad?'

'The Phipps Memorial Collection. Ducker Street,' said Mr Greeley, with careful distinctness.

'Oh, Ducker Street,' said the lad carelessly. 'Fourpence.'

'*Return*,' said Mr Greeley doggedly.

'Oh, return. Sempunce-'a-'pn'y.'

Mr Greeley already had the coins ready; he paid up and sank back into his own thoughts. Ducker Street! The conductor, had it seemed, heard of the street and not the Collection. Yet the street was a short one, a mere link between two main streets at the centre of the town, and there was hardly anything else there except the Collection. But it was the street you had to ask for. A triviality, yet a straw that showed how the wind blew. Forgetfulness, forgetfulness everywhere: the great days, the great doings, blown away on the gritty wind.

The bus halted at Ducker Street, and Mr Greeley got out and stood for a moment on the pavement. The Collection was beside the station, whose main entrance was two streets away. From the station Mr Greeley could hear the clash of wagons being shunted. Drawn by the sound, he hesitated. But what was the use? There was no hiss or chuff to be heard, not a plume of white to be seen; the station had been modernized and there were no steam locomotives working now. And diesels ... Mr Greeley had no objection to diesels in their own way, but there was no interest in watching them. Who wanted to watch a lot of steel boxes moving about?

He went up the steps of the Collection and hurried in. The large, whitewashed building was not very warm, but it seemed so after the chill of the street, and it was possible to take off one's overcoat without discomfort. Mr Greeley did so, but kept on his cap and muffler. Hanging up his macintosh, he turned to greet the attendant who usually sat on a chair just inside the door, a taciturn, grizzled man whom he had grown to like. But instead of the familiar attendant, a new and youthful face looked at him from under a peaked cap.

'Where's Ernie?' Mr Greeley asked.

'He's off sick,' the stripling replied. 'I'm doing his job till he gets back.' He made no further explanation of himself: what his normal job was, where his peaked cap came from (Ernie never wore one), and how he could be spared to take over from Ernie. Was he a trainee? Was Ernie's job being kept warm for him? He was a non-explainer, a budding authoritarian. Mistrusting him, Mr Greeley moved away.

Never mind! Attendant or no attendant, here she was, and here she would always be. The Phipps Collection was not very large; a few old wagons, a glass case or two containing old railwaymen's uniforms and tools, a couple of narrow-gauge engines standing one behind the other on a stretch of antique track, and a number of scale models of historic engines, some of which, if you fed them a penny, whirred sadly into motion for a little while. But all these were accompaniments, grouped on the margin. The pride of the Collection, the one big, important item that made it worth calling a Collection at all, stood firmly in the middle. Her brass gleamed, her paint shone, her majestic size drew the eye of everyone who entered. She was a gigantic green-and-gold engine of the 4–6–0 type, complete with her eight-wheeled tender. Over her huge driving wheels, brass letters proclaimed her official name, which was that of a castle. But Mr Greeley, in the years when he and this giantess had lived their lives together, had always called her Daisy. He could not have said why; Daisy just seemed to suit her. In his long dialogues with her, as she swayed and hissed and thundered, and the riveted metal plates shivered under his feet, Mr Greeley had simply found himself calling her Daisy, and that was that.

He drew his hand along the edge of her long platform.

'Hello, Daisy,' he said softly. 'Another morning, old girl.' Daisy stood impassively: she had no means of replying. Yet Mr Greeley did not feel that it was artificial, or even eccentric, to speak to her. Their relationship had been a living one: he had fed strength into her veins, caused her to leap and sway, heaving hundreds of tons of solid matter into urgent, clattering motion. And at the end of the run his hand had shut off her steam, calmed her, cradled her into her metallic sleep. And now she was sleeping for ever. But he was too sensible a man to fight against his own subjective feelings, and his feelings told him that he was her driver, and would always be her driver, and to her he could never be as other men were.

Stiffly, Mr Greeley clambered up Daisy's steps and into that cab in which he had spent thousands of hours. Taking out a soft duster, he carefully polished the brass fittings that made up Daisy's intelligence, her nerve centre, the seat of her personality. Then he straightened up and took a long, calm look out of the window, first on the platform side, then on the off side.

All was clear. Except for a small, meaningless commotion on the floor of the Collection. A little figure, with jerky movements, looking like an insect beside the monumental locomotive, was scurrying towards them. It was the new attendant.

'No standing on the exhibits, please,' he barked, hurrying. Drawing near, his face came to the level of Mr Greeley's boots. 'I must have you down, please.'

'Down?' said Mr Greeley incredulously. Could he believe what his ears told him? *Down?* Him?

'There's a notice up,' said the youth firmly. 'We can't allow the public to climb up on the exhibits.'

'I'm not the public, lad,' said Mr Greeley. 'I was this engine's regular driver in the last thirty years of her life.' He spoke forgivingly: after all, it was the boy's first day on the job.

'Please come *down*,' the young attendant repeated. His face was pale and stern: he might have been defending the grey head of a parent against outrage. The Collection might have been a cathedral, in danger from a barbaric horde. 'Look, the regulations – '

'Fetch the Superintendent,' Mr Greely commanded loudly. 'Go on, fetch him! I won't deal with you!'

At this moment the Superintendent, roused by the sound of their voices, appeared at the door of his office. Having many other duties, he spent only two days a week at the Collection: but this was one of his days, and Mr Greeley knew that it was.

'What's the trouble, Perkins?' he asked, taking off his glasses with a weary gesture that was characteristic of him. He was a tall, distinguished-looking man, prematurely white-haired, and with that air of polite absence of mind that grows on museum officials. He could be softly polite to whomsoever he was listening or talking to, while at the same time demonstrably thinking of something else.

'Public climbing on the exhibits, sir,' said Perkins stiffly. He stood like a lance-corporal.

'Dear me,' said the Superintendent gently. 'That's not the public, it's Mr Greeley. He spent so long in the cab of that engine that we make an exception for him. How are you today, Mr Greeley?'

'I'm in good shape, Superintendent,' Mr Greeley smiled. 'But Daisy's in better.'

The Superintendent nodded gravely. His mind was already back in his office, looking at balance-sheets. 'All the better for seeing you, Mr Greeley,' he said, and turned to go back.

'My mistake, sir,' said Perkins, challenging the Superintendent to make some wrapping-up comment.

'We all make them, Perkins,' said the Superintendent vaguely. The reply did not satisfy Perkins, who had expected to be absolved, and into the bargain congratulated on his zeal. He glared briefly at Mr Greeley, then turned and walked away after the Superintendent.

'*Public*,' said Mr Greeley to Daisy, bitterly 'I hope we can get Ernie back. He knows what's what.' He polished some of Daisy's array of brass tubes. '*You* don't think I'm the public, eh, old girl?'

Mr Greeley's calm had been badly shaken, but half an hour of tranquil communion with Daisy restored it. Stepping briskly, he went across the street to The Viaduct, a public house he had frequented for fifty years. There, he enjoyed his usual midday meal: a pint of beer and a sandwich. As he ate, and took slow, meditative pulls at his beer, Mr Greeley looked round at the juke-box, the tubular steel furniture, the pornographic advertisements for non-alcoholic drinks. The place had changed beyond recognition. He had known it when it was a classic railwayman's pub. Hard-working shunters and oilers, yes, even humble porters in their shorn-off jackets, had rubbed shoulders at that bar with the drivers of famous trains. Including Mr Greeley himself. Often and often had he come striding quickly into the pub with a raging thirst, flinging down on the polished bar a handful of small change that was almost too hot to hold. The fierce heat from Daisy's firebox used to make his overalls so hot they were all but scorched. And how he had sweated! And with what lovely, prodigal gulps had he poured down his throat pints, quarts, yes, even a gallon on occasion, of the good beer always on tap at The Viaduct!

The beer seemed to have lost its flavour these days. But then, Mr Greeley reflected, he did not come to it straight from Daisy's cab, with his senses drugged by speed and roaring wind, his skin wet and his throat dry. Beer! It was not just beer in those days, it was a benediction. Sighing, but inwardly happy because strengthened and warmed by these memories, Mr Greeley drank the last inch of his weak, flat pint and walked to the door, nodding to the licensee.

Back at the Collection, Mr Greeley swung himself, once more, up the steps to Daisy's cab. From up here, the world looked sane and comely. Even if there was no track stretching ahead, even if all you could see was the flat concrete floor of the Collection, and opposite you the whitewashed brick wall. Well, that was how the world had gone. It had shrunk, and become flat and grey and washed-out. But at least he and Daisy were both still here.

'Nobody'll ever drive you again, old girl,' he said to her, bending his head so that his voice lingered intimately about her proud immobile controls. 'I was the last, and I saw you out. And I was the only one that knew what you could really do. When you *wanted* to, that is, old Daisy!'

Silently, in his mind, he rehearsed the beloved statistics. Heating surface, two thousand and fifty square feet. Weight, fifty-eight tons seventeen hundredweight. The figures gleamed in his mind like the words of some immortal lyric. In their hedged-in statements they contained the whole of his working life: fifty years of eye and sinew. Work is the misfortune of Adam, laid on man by a vengeful God: Mr Greeley in his time had cursed the alarm clock, coughed on dark mornings, ached as he waited at the icy bus-stop: but never once had he climbed up into Daisy's cab without a flicker of life-giving excitement, a quickening nervous tremor at the root of his heart.

A suppressed burst of tittering, not quite so suppressed as

to be inaudible to his old ears, caused Mr Greeley to look up from his reverie. Standing by Daisy's front buffers, peering round at his face as it was framed in the driver's window, stood two children, a girl of perhaps ten and a boy some three years older.

'*Now* can you hear him?' the girl asked her brother. Mr Greeley guessed that she had overheard him talking to himself, and wanted her brother to share this exquisite joke.

Seeing Mr Greeley's eye on him, the boy dropped all furtiveness and came boldly along beside Daisy's driving-wheels, which towered above him with their imperious height of nearly six feet. He looked directly into Mr Greeley's face, as if about to start a conversation.

Mr Greeley, forgiving the girlish insolence of the sister, smiled benignly down. The boy reminded him of so many similar boys, school-capped and macintoshed, over the years. How they had longed for a few words with the driver of a crack locomotive! And even now, even in the shorn glory of the Collection, it seemed that the feeling was still alive.

'Nice engine, isn't she?' he volunteered, to help the boy over his shyness. 'I was her driver. She was built in 1914. I was built some time before that, so I'm older'n she is.' He smiled warmly. Then he noticed the boy's eyes. They were like two stones.

'Anything up to two hundred tons, we used to pull,' Mr Greeley proffered. Then, under the stare of those two utterly unforgiving eyes, he stopped and turned away. What was the use? The boy was beyond his gravitational pull. What had drawn him to visit the Collection at all, Mr Greeley could not imagine. What *was* clear was his complete and final unwillingness to consider Mr Greeley as a living being of the same species as himself. Contempt, backed by a hard curiosity, had been the message of those eyes. Instead of feeling any thrill at finding himself in the presence of a man who had driven a locomotive capable of hauling two hundred tons, shooting steam high into the air, thrusting and drumming with all that wonderful lyric energy, the boy had behaved more like a particular heartless biologist noting the reactions of some repulsive creature under vivisection.

Mr Greeley sighed. He did not understand the world as it was now. Perhaps he had never understood it very well. Daisy had been his means of understanding the world; she had translated all experience into terms of load, gradient, pressure, curves and adhesion. So arranged, he had been able to grasp it and make sense of it. And boys like this one with his hard blue eyes, escaped from their prosperous homes on Christmas-holiday or August excursions, had recognized his authority and bowed to it. But now . . . well, everything passed. Daisy was younger than he was, but their working life had ended at the same time. Only her museum-life, that long lonely twilight, would go on longer than his. But let no child look at her as this one had looked at him!

Climbing sadly down, Mr Greeley passed an hour listlessly peering at the other exhibits in the Collection. Shadows began to gather: the misguided young attendant, loftily ignored by Mr Greeley, switched on the lighting.

It was almost time to go back and face his daughter and her family. For some reason Mr Greeley found it even more difficult than usual to accept this necessity. He felt a blind urge to hide himself in some dark corner of the Collection, wait till everyone had gone home, and then come out and spend the night in blissful, unhampered converse with Daisy. But he knew such thoughts were fantastic. At half past five, he fetched his overcoat, put it on and buttoned it. Then, quickly, he mounted Daisy's steps one more time.

'Don't worry, girl,' he admonished her. 'They'll learn. They'll respect you if they don't respect me. And I'm quite happy, see? I don't matter, you know.' He smoothed his hand gently over her brass wheels and levers. 'Good night, old Daisy,' he said.

Outside, the street was dark. Mr Greeley had to wait a long time for a bus. A light, almost freezing rain was falling. Back at Mrs Foster's house, he had very little appetite for supper.

'You generally like egg and chips, father,' said Mrs Foster reproachfully.

'Can I have Grandad's?' asked her watchful son.

'I think I'll turn in,' said Mr Greeley.

Lying in his narrow bed, Mr Greeley felt that his bones were weightless, airy. Rising, he slumbered near the ceiling. The wind that stirred the curtain's edge caused him to waver. Then, through air that rocked like water, he was at the bus-stop again. A bus was already waiting.

'The Collection,' said Mr Greeley firmly, holding out a golden sovereign.

'Sorry, you'll have to ask the driver,' said the conductor with the faintest hint of condescension. Without wasting words on him, Mr Greeley moved straight up to where a small window gave access to the driver. Poking his head in, Mr Greeley hissed into the driver's ear, 'The Collection'.

'Where's that?' said the driver, half turning in his seat. He turned no further, because Mr Greeley's powerful hands came through the aperture and gripped his throat.

The driver choked and struggled, but Mr Greeley said, 'Follow my directions. Straight on here. Left here. Round this crossing. Right here, and right again.' His fingers twined lovingly round the driver's windpipe. The driver, well-fleshed and soft to the touch, drove with imploring care. Passengers at intermediate stops were left bewildered and abandoned.

The bus reached Ducker Street, slowed, and stopped. Only then did Mr Greeley unclasp his hands from the driver's plump throat.

'Remember next time, mate,' he said grimly. 'When someone says the Collection, go there and no messing.'

He left the bus with stiff dignity and walked up the steps and into the Collection. It was closed, empty and silent, but a bright moon hung in the sky, and for some reason was able to shine straight down on to the pale concrete floor. Looking up, Mr Greeley saw that the roof of the Collection had gone. The building was open to the warm summer night: for summer had abruptly supplanted winter during the wild and perilous bus ride.

Soft air caressed the engines, the trucks, the lamps and uniforms, the glass cases. Daisy's brasswork gleamed triumphantly in the mellow light. Seen under the moon, she seemed more colossal than in daylight.

Mr Greeley hurried across the floor of the Collection and climbed into Daisy's cab.

'Steam up, by Heaven!' he exclaimed in excitement.

Daisy's firebox glowed hot, her pipes sang, the needles of her pressure gauge crept slowly round from left to right.

Then Mr Greeley noticed that his overalls and his shiny black leather cap were hanging in the corner of the cab, on the hook where he had always hung them.

'We're due out!' he said. All at once it came back to him. 'The seven-fifty down!'

His hands, steady and capable, went out to Daisy's heavy brass controls. A few calculated turns on this wheel, a sharp downward pull on that lever. The wheels came into motion. Daisy's whole frame heaved and shook with excitement as her massive connecting-rods began to slide back and forth.

'Where's Ginger?' Mr Greeley asked irritably. He looked round for the fireman he had had on his first runs in 1920. Then he remembered. It wasn't Ginger, it was young Herbert. Or was it Harry Jackson? the last one?

Twisting round, he saw a figure crouched beside the coal, shovel in hand. The stance was Harry Jackson's. That was how Harry had always stood, shovel at the ready, one calculating eye on the firebox. But the face was Ginger's.

'You've come back, Ginger,' said Mr Greeley calmly.

'Yes, gaffer,' said Ginger. 'I wanted to be by the firebox again. It's cold out there.'

Out where? Mr Greeley wondered. But he turned his attention to the controls again. Daisy was rising easily into the air, floating steadily upwards. The Collection fell away behind them, and Mr Greeley thought he glimpsed the Superintendent standing alone in the space Daisy had occupied, looking up at them wonderingly, fumbling in his upper pocket for his glasses.

Then there was a jolt as Daisy's wheels hit the track. There it was, stretching ahead of them in the glorious moonlight – a mile, three miles, five, ten miles of straight rails.

'The road!' Mr Greeley breathed. He fed Daisy more pressure. And more. And more. The miles whipped by, and Mr Greeley and Ginger shouted for joy in the shuddering cab.

'She's pulling a treat!' Ginger called.

'Clean!' Mr Greeley shouted.

He remembered now. Daisy had been in for servicing. Her boiler had been scraped out. He could never understand why clean water left so much deposit, but it did. Well, they had done a fine job. She had never pulled more smoothly.

'A hundred and seventy,' said Mr Greeley to himself, looking at the pressure gauge. 'Well, why not?' And he increased the pressure till the needle stood at a hundred and eighty.

'Better stop there,' said Mr Greeley. He peered ahead through his window. The track stretched away into an inviting landscape of trees and fields. No curves of less than two miles' radius on the whole stretch. He remembered it; his favourite run. But what was different about it? Oh, yes – the housing estates had gone. These woods and meadows had been gradually shovelled away, during the years he and Daisy had travelled that road, and hundreds of little brick boxes had sprung up, connected by concrete ribbons and towered over by glaring arc-lights. Now, all that was gone, the trees waved softly in the moonlight and threw their shadows on to the broad fields. Mr Greeley blew Daisy's whistle, and he could imagine the sound echoing to lonely farmhouses along with the bark of a fox and the cry of an owl.

But of course, it was no mystery. The time that had bowed him to old age was rolled back, he and Daisy were young again, the trees had not been cut down and the meadows still gleamed under the moon. Rolling up his sleeves, Mr Greeley noticed at once his arms were more fully fleshed. The stringy old man's muscles had rounded out into the firm, contoured strength he had once taken for granted. And all at once Mr Greeley knew that he would never be old again. He stood straighter, he saw more clearly. Daisy, in all her thundering power and bulk, seemed to submit to him like a bride. And back home, he knew, Marion waited for him. This evening, at the end of the run back, he would get the bus home and Marion would be waiting. He would take off his working clothes, and wash, and eat, and later that night they would love each other as they used to do.

Daisy rolled easily along at sixty miles an hour, her pressure steady at a hundred and eighty. The track went into a long, full-speed curve, and Mr Greeley took the opportunity to look back and see the train they were pulling. Twelve coaches and a guard's van.

'Thirteen,' said Mr Greeley and grinned. That was a super-stition that had never bothered him.

Daisy's smoke plumed above them, the steel plates shud-dered beneath, the dark trees flew by, and the wind roared past their ears. Ginger leaned on his shovel, and he and Mr Greeley grinned at each other with utter contentment. Soon the run would be over; in some unexplained way, in fact, they were already on the return trip, and Marion would be putting the pie in the oven and beginning to watch for the bus that would bring him home. Home? Home.

Standing over Mr Greeley, the young doctor shook his head to Mrs Foster and her husband.

'His resistance is weak,' he said. 'You can't expect anything else at his age. We can get him into an oxygen tent, and he might rally or he might not.' He rubbed his eyes. It was a continual annoyance to him that people seemed to wait for his turn on night-duty before deciding to die. Why couldn't they die at week-ends?

'We must do everything we can, of course,' said Cyril Foster. Inside, he felt a sensation of lightness and relief of which he had the grace to feel slightly ashamed. With the old man gone, that back room could be very useful. The children could have it as a rumpus room. They'd always wanted a rumpus room.

Things happened very quickly after that. Mrs Foster shed a few genuine tears. Their eldest child, Arlene, appeared on the landing and was shooed back to bed by Mr Foster.

'Poor old dad,' Mrs Foster whimpered. 'They didn't keep any heating on in that place.'

'Course of nature; seventy-five years is a long time,' said the doctor.

'Good night, old Daisy,' said Mr Greeley.

The ambulance arrived. Mr Foster went down and opened the door. The ambulance men joked as they came up the stairs. They got Mr Greeley on to a stretcher and carefully started to go back the way they had come. Arlene appeared again and was whisked back to bed by Mrs Foster. Mr Greeley died. Mr Foster held the front door open as the ambulance men carried the stretcher gently out. The doctor said, 'He may rally or he may not.'

And the great locomotive, standing silent and imprisoned on the cold grey floor of the Collection, entered another phase of its history.

Giles and Penelope

'But look, surely,' said Giles. 'Theatre of Cruelty isn't just a simple release from restraints. On the contrary. It bears all the marks of a complex consciousness trying to get back to simplicity and disintegrating in the process.'

'Yes, but what kind of simplicity?' Penelope insisted on her question, though her voice remained, as it always did, quiet and well modulated. She was not the kind of girl who indulged in shrill, intellectual arguments, audible at every table of the small, hot restaurants in which they took place. She knew that that kind of girl had gone out. Loud, impassioned voices were as dead as the long overcoat; that was what Giles said, and Giles was right.

'Of course, cruelty doesn't matter one way or the other,' said Giles. He picked up the menu and stared greedily at it through his thick, black-framed glasses. 'It's just a stage. A necessary stage in the process of disintegration. A machine has to be taken to pieces before it can be reassembled. What the Theatre of Cruelty really shows – ' he looked up from the menu, suddenly convinced of his own seriousness '– is that the disintegration isn't completed yet.'

Meanwhile, *vive la cruauté*, Penelope said to herself. She moved her empty sherry-glass carefully away from the edge of the table. She loved Giles, and it was sweet of him to insist on this weekly treat. But the small, unsmotherable fact was that she preferred eating in the flat, even though she had all the bother of cooking and washing up. Giles planned everything; his life was carefully thought out. Once a week he took her to dinner in a good restaurant and made the sort of intelligent conversation to her that he used to make when they first knew each other, in that brief halcyon period before she had gone to live with him. 'Heavens,' he used to say, 'if we don't do *something* to counteract the dailiness, we'll end up sitting and staring at each other as if we were *married* or something,' and Penelope had dutifully laughed, her soft rippling acquiescence confirming his judgement that nothing could be more absurd than marriage.

The waiter, having left them time to get through their drinks and study the menu, now approached with beautiful satiric deference. Giles made a show of consulting Penelope as he ordered the meal stage by stage, though it was clear that his mind was made up; and in any case, after a year together, he knew her taste in food as well as his own. It was as if (Penelope caught herself guiltily harbouring the thought) he were reconstructing, from memory, the way a man treats a girl during the stage when he is making a play for her, testing her out, estimating the solidity of the ground before each footstep.

Now, still with that suggestion of acting from memory, he took his glasses off with a dignified gesture, suggesting responsible weariness about to relax and enjoy life; and asked her, with a kind smile, 'Anything interesting at work today?'

Penelope was twenty-five. At the time when she met Giles, her thoughts had begun to run on marriage and security. In fact, part of her motive in going to live with Giles had been the unspoken, unformulated, barely perceptible notion that some sort of regular relationship with a man might turn her into a wife, inwardly at least, and that if they were happy together they might find themselves absent-mindedly wandering, one fine Saturday, over the doorstep of a Registry Office. Yet here she was, at twenty-five, with the girlishness of her beauty at the exact moment of strengthening and thickening into the beauty of a mature woman. And she was working on the *Daily* – the name is immaterial. A slick, shrill, mass-circulation sheet devoted to the processing of news into snobbery and the transitory excitement of passions.

'It'll bring you into contact with life,' Giles had said, pushing her with soft persistence into taking the job. 'A few years in the reporters' room on a paper like that and you'll have seen the heart-beat of our time, really seen it, not just listened to it through a stethoscope like the rest of us.'

The metaphor, at the time, had seemed compelling. Penelope

had had too much respect for Giles's assessment of life to stop and ask him why it was better diagnostic practice to watch a heart-beat rather than listen to it. Nor had the sensation of closeness to the inner spirit of the age, the vocation of bedpan-carrier to the ailing *Zeitgeist*, survived a year in the offices of this daily. What she felt close to was nothing more interesting than haste, greed for money, cynicism and a kind of battered hankering for something that would never happen.

'Interesting, well,' she said, wrinkling her soft forehead. 'There was a big conference about boosting circulation. We humble reporters weren't asked to it, but we shall feel the results of it all right. Apparently the circulation department's been absolutely *demanding* some action – *anything* as long as it leads to an increase.'

'It'll be interesting to see what they come up with,' said Giles. Himself employed in the research department of a large inter-national organization, constantly looking up facts in reference books and sometimes making telephone calls in foreign lan-guages, he felt himself impeccably intellectual, and able to afford a large tolerance towards the mass media and its denizens.

Penelope felt herself squirming with resentment like a school-girl. At such moments she hated her dependence on Giles. He was so contentedly aloof, so certain that she needed – or, at any rate, was going to get – no higher place in the scheme of things than to scuttle about in a pool, shredding garbage with specially designed claws, while he peered from time to time, with patronizing interest, into the depths.

'It doesn't add up to a very pleasant life,' she said reasonably, 'knowing that the object of what you're doing is not to inform people or to make them more responsible about what's going on, but just to set baits for them, the old baits of sex and violence.'

'Look at it in another perspective,' said Giles, glancing about for the waiter, 'and you'll see it more hopefully. It's all a part of that calculated disintegration that we need.'

'So I'm contributing to the cosmic Theatre of Cruelty?' she murmured ironically.

'Quite so,' said Giles, and before she could tax him with

missing her irony the waiter was at their table with the first course, and the meal blanketed their discussion with its clogging insistence.

When it was finally over, Giles lit a small cigar and, as he waved out the match, said, 'Well, let's move on to the party.'

Penelope had been waiting for the words. After their weekly dining-out, Giles invariably knew of 'a party' to which they could 'move on' – a formulation he as invariably employed. Giles knew a lot of people, all of whom gave a lot of parties. Some of these parties were small and intimate, with the personalities of the guests carefully orchestrated, so that it would be a pity to disrupt the harmony by not turning up. Others were large, noisy and undiscriminating, and bound to be attended by a number of people who had not been invited: so that it would be 'amusing' to look in, 'a pity' to miss the chance of an unlooked-for encounter with a friend one had lost track of. And then there was always the chance of making some new acquaintance with an interesting person. Giles's rationality, his air of sensible completeness, was developed almost to the point of self-parody. 'Oh, I'm very organized, I know,' he would say, beaming his self-satisfaction through those overbearingly heavy glasses. 'I can't help it – I was born like that.' And she, Penelope, waiting glumly to be carried to yet another in the long series of parties that made up Giles's recreational life, like a gaily gesticulatory dado round the walls of a sensible modern nursery, felt again the old hopeless sense of being organized, assigned without consultation to her place and function: in a word used.

This time, she thought in the taxi, she would break out. Find a man, flirt heavily, make Giles jealous. She was pretty enough to gather up a male at any party she went to, and if she threw herself into the act, giving the convincing impression of a woman in the opening stages of a serious involvement, she could hold him for the entire evening. Let Giles feel uneasy; let him feel that his calculations were going wrong, that an article of his carefully chosen furniture had got up and started walking from room to room; let him scowl, sulk, finally break out with reproaches. Yes, to see Giles reproachful would be satisfaction to her. His accustomed air of omnicompetent good humour would be wiped away for one evening at least, and she would feel like a human being again.

They arrived; the hostess, having shown them where to put their coats and given them each a glass of some unidentifiable liquid, left them to sink or swim in the choppy sea of the party. Penelope walked away from Giles at once, instead of waiting for him to drift away as he usually did, immersing himself more and more in sociabilities until he finally crossed the line, at some imperceptible point, between being with her and not being with her. This time, she threw one raking look round the room, recognized a face she knew, and made for it without hesitation.

Ordinarily, her choice would not have fallen on Leonard Smith. For one thing, he worked on her newspaper, so that his face was a perpetual reminder of that servitude which had made her accept life on Giles's terms rather than her own. Then there were more personal reasons. Leonard Smith had been in Fleet Street for twenty years, processing information into little tablets to be swallowed by people whom he despised. He never thought of the paper's readers without contempt; which meant, since he spent his days and nights working for those readers, that he never thought of himself without contempt. This self-loathing had turned Leonard Smith's blood sour, his face leathery, his eye cold and sceptical. Married to a disillusioned shrew, he seldom went home, and gave the impression of living on meat pie and baked beans in side-street restaurants with steamed-up windows. Knowing exactly what his work amounted to, he had still nothing to put in its place, and consequently was thought to be a reliable man and often taken into the confidence of his employers.

Even in her present mood, Penelope could not have brought herself to use Leonard Smith as the sole instrument for goading Giles into jealousy. Her motive in beginning a conversation with him was nothing more than the wish to find a point of entry into the solid wall of strangers, a point chosen by herself and not by Giles. If she began by talking to Leonard Smith, she would presumably progress to talking to other people. Leonard Smith, however, seemed not to understand this. Seeing Penelope make straight for him, he evidently gained the impression that she wanted a *tête-à-tête*. With an ochreous glow in the depths of his weary eyes that must have indicated satisfaction of some kind, he talked. She made perfunctory replies, and glanced about. He ignored the glances and talked on. About the office, and recent developments at the office, and what the immediate future would bring about at the office, and what the Sales Manager had said to the Features Editor at the office.

In desperation, Penelope looked round for Giles and saw, with a hard ball in the pit of her stomach, that he was talking and smiling confidently to two attractive girls, both of whom were looking at him with interest. Perhaps he was giving them a new perspective on the Theatre of Cruelty. Penelope longed to shake free of Leonard Smith, and was opening her mouth to utter some excuse, when she became aware of what he was saying.

'So it's the old I-talked-to routine again. And this time it's got to be a tart. Either a call-girl, or one of the cheaper girls out of one of those dives or on the street. And I'm afraid that's where you come in, Penelope.'

He was looking at her with feigned jocular casualness, behind which his eyes were steady and intent, measuring her reaction.

'I – come in?'

He nodded. 'Features handed it to me to set up. You know – find that girl and tee it up, pay her something for her time and all that. They'll see to the pictures themselves – phoney ones, of course. But – ' He leaned forward, no longer concealing that he was eyeing her closely. 'One thing they're set on. A girl does the story.'

'A girl?'

'One of the young lady reporters must do the actual interview and write it up,' he mouthed with an insulting over-precision.

'But why, why?'

'All sorts of reasons,' said Leonard Smith. His face had become closed, secretive. 'Some of 'em are real reasons, some phoney. One real reason – and one's enough – would be that a girl, if she went at it the right way, would probably get more material. These girls are so used to playing men along – if they talk to a man, they tell him the same as they tell any other man. Just what he wants to hear.'

'Well, I hope – ' Penelope began and stopped.

'You hope what?' Leonard Smith demanded. There was a thin, vulpine eagerness in his voice. Suddenly she knew: he wants to stain me, and this is his only way.

'It's all been settled, my love,' purred Leonard Smith. 'Some of the girls are too squeamish. Others – well, they're such little tarts themselves, they wouldn't know what to ask the girl. You're the only one. Sympathetic, interested in people. You're a nice girl and you also – know the score.' His voice dropped, very slightly, on these last three words; it became confiding; it said, 'You know what it is to have lovers, even though they don't pay you.'

Penelope struggled to hold her voice steady. 'You've picked on a – girl for this interview?'

'I've picked you.'

'No, no, I mean – a girl to *be* interviewed.' For some reason she could not, with Leonard Smith's eyes on her, bring out the word 'whore', and 'prostitute' sounded prudishly stuffy and statistical.

'I've picked one. She's called, or rather she calls herself Tania and she operates in the Victoria area. I suspect her real name is something like Ethel. She's a girl of about your age. You'll like her.'

'Did you just go out at random and find her? Or was she – a previous acquaintance?'

'That's kind of a personal question,' said Leonard Smith. He was enjoying himself hugely. Whether his dealings with prostitutes went on only in the crevices of his unswept imagination or whether, with his unhappy home life and his journalistically ravenous instincts, he spent half his time in their scented apartments, she could form no idea. In either case, he was having a deliriously good time soldering Penelope firmly to the rock bottom of his prurient fantasies. Chance had put him in a position to wield power over her, and he was too alert to let slip such an opportunity for pleasure.

She bore it a few minutes longer, for no better reason than that she found it almost impossibly difficult to turn on her heel and walk away without uttering some more or less polite formula, and no formula would come. In the end, muttering something vague, she slipped away and spent the next three hours chattering frantically to any stranger whose mere presence would shield her against a renewal of Leonard Smith's persecution. Somehow, she managed to find the strength not to go up to Giles and implore him to take her home. She had never wanted to be the kind of girl who, at parties, made a fuss and demanded to be taken home. That kind of girl had gone out.

Going home in the taxi, she sat tensely beside Giles as the empty streets, lit but deserted like so many stage sets waiting for plays to begin, flowed past the window. The unreality of the city at this late hour, combined with fatigue, apprehension and alcohol, threw an air of fantasy over everything she perceived and gave her the sense of being in a dream. Giles talked on, his words spinning like an endless soft thread out of some cocoon of inviolable self-satisfaction; she answered mechanically, conscious of no relationship with him, feeling only that her life was moving in the wrong direction, that the powerful machine of Giles's needs and habits had drawn her into its meshes and was imposing on her a false rhythm, a false outline, a false momentum.

At home, Giles yawned, hung up his jacket, walked heavily into the bathroom, and quickly made for bed, where he lay on his back, breathing sibilantly through his nose. Penelope, moving awkwardly about the flat, knew that he was waiting for her. It was another of his habits. On the evenings when he took her out and treated her with that extra ceremony belonging to their bygone phase, he invariably, once in bed, turned on the sexual pressure higher than usual. It was – the thought occurred to her suddenly in all its brutal clarity – the return he naturally expected for his outlay of energy and money. Treated with the fresh delicacy due to a new girl-friend, she was expected to return that compliment with a renewed zest and inventiveness between the sheets. The thought chilled her as she fumbled with her clothing in front of the electric fire; stripping her body for his pleasure like a butcher laying out meat. And tomorrow ... She winced. All of a sudden she felt too vulnerable, too uncertain, to do what was asked of her, either here or at work. A prostitute had at least made her choice, plumped for a defined role, a position immediately recognizable. That made for strength. Whereas her own position, dragging herself to that newspaper office every morning, forcing her life out of its natural shape, to fit in with the wishes of a man who saw her merely as part of the furniture of his flat, of his life, of his emotions . . .?

'Don't be long, darling,' came the voice of Giles, slow and drugged with the warmth of the bed and the expectation of pleasure. Dread filled Penelope's heart as she pulled frozenly at the snaps and hooks of her underclothes. Naked, she pulled on her nightdress, and as she did so she caught herself huddling over towards the corner of the room, her back to the bed, so that Giles should not see her.

The realization finally came: it was hopeless. She knew that she must refuse him tonight. Surely it was her right? Their relationship was a free compact between them? She went over and sat on the bed, looking down at him.

'Giles.'

'Darling.'

'I want to sleep by myself tonight.'

His face snapped awake. It was almost comical. Drowsiness and sensuality were wiped away as if by a cloth, and instantly his features were full of resentment and wariness.

'Sleep by yourself? Where?'

She gestured helplessly. 'There's the spare bed.'

'But it's not made up.'

'I'll make it up,' she said flatly.

He sat upright. 'But why? Why, for God's sake?'

'Oh, just because.'

'It can't be the time of the month . . .'

'You know quite well it isn't.'

He tried coaxing. 'Come to bed, sweetheart. I know one gets these moods.'

'Yes, that's it. A mood.'

'But they don't last. Come to me.'

'This one will.'

Giles was angry. 'You sound very certain.'

'I don't mean it'll last long. I just mean I want to sleep by myself tonight, for once.'

'But *tonight* . . . I could understand it on an ordinary evening! But when we've been out, enjoying ourselves together . . .'

He's spent five pounds and now he wants five pounds' worth of fun.

She got off the bed and walked swiftly into the other room. As she made the bed, working quickly and shivering, she wondered whether he would follow her. But nothing happened, and soon she heard from his breathing that he was asleep. He had written off his five pounds: a man can't win all the time.

Still shivering, Penelope got into her solitary bed. To be left alone – that was something, at least. And this mood would pass; she would love Giles again. Or perhaps she would not. And if it was over, what then? She tried to imagine her life, going back to living alone, going back to that state of never-ending unconscious vigilance, looking in every street, every office, every party, for the man who was to appear out of nowhere and lay her unhappiness to rest.

She slept, though the losing of consciousness meant nothing more than the passing from one trance to another. One moment she was lying tensely in her bed, the next she was walking up a flight of stairs and confronting a door on which was pinned a card: FRENCH MODEL AVAILABLE.

In her dream, Penelope floated through this door and was immediately in the middle of her conversation with the prostitute whom Leonard Smith had found for her. The girl was as he had said, of about her own age; expensively dressed, with an elaborate fluffed-out coiffure and a cheerful, unthinking face, so that the thought immediately formed itself: she seems to have nothing behind her eyes.

'Ask me anything you like, dear,' the girl said. 'I'm quite used to talking about it.' And she smiled encouragingly. But Penelope could think of nothing to ask.

'Giles sent me,' she volunteered, at last.

The girl smiled encouragingly. 'I don't know Giles,' she said, 'but I know all about him.'

'How?' Penelope faltered.

'Well, you see, I know everything. I know the men's thoughts before they think them.' As she spoke, the prostitute grew broader, lines appeared round her eyes and mouth, and her jowls took on a pendulous fullness. 'I'm fifty. I knew Giles's father and I knew Giles when he was a little boy.'

'You're his mother!' Penelope was on her feet, frightened, accusing.

'No,' the woman laughed. 'He had one of his own, he didn't need me for that. But he used to come and see me, often, when he was growing up. I taught him – you know, everything. You know what I mean, dear. You're his wife, aren't you?'

Penelope nodded. 'Yes. I didn't really want us to get married, but Giles insisted.'

The woman leaned forward. Her skin had wrinkled still more as they talked, and huge crusted rings had appeared on her fingers: she was like a bejewelled toad.

'Well, it's a funny thing you should say that. He was very set on marrying his mother. He came and talked all about it to me. He said no other woman could make him so happy, and he'd always wanted to, you know, have sex with her but she wouldn't, not without they got married. Well, I encouraged him. I knew they'd be very happy together. And he was going ahead with it too. They were nearly at the altar. And then his mother threw him over, quite sudden, just like that. She married his father instead.'

Penelope shifted uncomfortably in her chair. Suddenly she felt as if her nervous system had been flooded with light.

'I know,' she said coolly. 'As a matter of fact, I was behind the scenes all the time. You wouldn't understand, being too closely involved with Giles. But for your information, the key to the whole thing was his mother's name.'

'Her name?' the woman cried. Suspicion peered from her eyes; even her nostrils and mouth looked wary.

'Yes. You see, she called herself Tania. But everybody knew her real name was Alice. I mean Ethel.'

As she stumbled over the names, Penelope's confidence ebbed away with hideous abruptness. The prostitute smiled, and kittenishly coiled her legs beneath her on the soft cushions. Her wrinkles and pendulous flesh disappeared; her face became youthful, her body lissom. She was twenty, no, eighteen. The uncomprehending scornfulness of youth stabbed at Penelope from her eyes.

'Alice! Ethel! A fat lot *you* know about it. Listen, put *this* in the paper. I have a good time. I like men, and they like me, and they give me what I want – *whatever it is*.' Exulting, and now of an unbearably radiant beauty, the girl stood up and pointed to the door. 'And please get out. I'm expecting somebody a lot more interesting than you. And a lot richer! You can make the rest up out of your imagination – you're good at that, aren't you? And you've got plenty of time to sit about in the office, thinking about it all.' As she spoke the girl shrank and her face became more childlike; she retreated to the very brink of puberty, and long golden pigtails sprang from her head. 'Giles likes them very young,' she pouted. 'He brings me dolls to play with.' Before Penelope's horrified eyes, she produced a doll which was a perfect miniature replica of Giles, made of sponge rubber, and began to fondle it. 'Leave me alone with my dolly, my Giles-dolly,' she lisped affectedly. Penelope was too shaken by terror and disgust to do anything but wake up. Lying rigid in her narrow bed, she forced herself to come back to complete consciousness, naming the objects in the room, which were just visible in the faint light from the window. Chest-of-drawers, framed Picasso print, trousers-press, tell me I was only dreaming. Slowly, painfully, she forced the images out of her mind, and in the blank emptiness that followed, true sleep came at last.

When she woke in the morning, her first impression was of the strangeness of her surroundings: this room, this bed, no one beside her. And, as memory came back, the strangeness persisted. She knew why she was there, instead of in Giles's bed, but still she had the sense of perceiving her life from a new angle and through a new lens. Lying back and stretching out her limbs, Penelope felt, a little, as she imagined a woman must feel who has given birth. Something she had been carrying was no longer with her. In its place was an emptiness, a tough, terrible sheath enclosing nothing.

Giles came in, dressing. He always set out in good time for work. He looked at her inquiringly as he knotted his tie.

'Are you getting up?' he asked, in a carefully neutral voice.

'No.'

'But work . . .?'

'I'm not going to work.'

He stood over her and looked down searchingly into her composed face. 'Shall I ring up and say you're ill?'

'If you like.'

'But,' he persisted, 'is something the matter?'

'Nothing's the matter. I'm just not going to work.'

'But why?'

Under the bedclothes, she gave a faint shrug. 'I've had enough of work.'

Anger flashed into his face. 'We could all say that, I suppose.'

'All right, let's all say it.'

He walked rapidly out of the room. She heard him bumping about in the kitchen, the tap splashed, the gas-stove popped, and soon he was back with two mugs of coffee. Without speaking, he handed her one, and she propped herself on one elbow to drink it.

'Now,' he said, sitting down on the bed. 'Tell me what this is all about.'

'Why has it got to be about something? I'm just not going back to work, that's all. I don't like it and I'm going to give up doing things I don't like.'

'And you honestly think life's like that? That you'll be able to get by without doing anything you don't want to do?'

She peered indifferently into the steam of her coffee. 'I'll try anyway.'

Giles said nothing more. He dressed quickly and left the house. When the door closed behind him, Penelope got out of bed immediately and wrapped the telephone in two blankets and her heaviest overcoat. Any time now, the paper would be trying to get her; perhaps Leonard Smith himself, wanting to know how she had slipped through the net he had woven for her. In its cocoon, the telephone's menacing ring would be audible, if at all, only as a harmless cricket-chirp. She went back to bed, slept calmly for an hour, then got up and had a long bath, tipping in the expensive crystals till the water bubbled with money. Soaping and stretching, she admired her own slim beauty. Why take this to work? Make it ride in crowded lifts, fight the rush-hour, breathe stale office air?

The day passed easily. Hungry at noon, she strolled to the near-by shops and spent all the money she had on food and a bottle of good wine. People hurried past, blinking in the winter sunshine; Penelope walked slowly, savouring leisure, hesitating deliciously over each purchase.

After eating, she cleared up the flat. In this mood, only elegance must surround her. Humming, she arranged flowers and cushions, moved chairs, straightened pictures on the walls. Then, dissatisfied with her surroundings, she moved on to the serious business of dressing. Her wardrobe dissatisfied her, but there would be time to choose new clothes later. Meanwhile, she carefully chose a dress, stockings, shoes, and spent unlimited time over make-up and hair. All this took until Giles arrived back; she had barely settled herself comfortably with a drink when his key turned in the lock.

He walked in, stopped and stared at her in astonishment. 'Have you been in all day?'

'I went out shopping for a bit.'

'And that's all you did? Go out shopping?'

'It's all I felt like doing.'

He put his brief-case down with a thud. 'Look here, Penelope, what's come over you?'

'I'll tell you,' she said levelly. 'I've decided to stop being a mug. If you want me to stay here with you, I'll stay. But I won't work as well. You can pay the bills, and you can give me an allowance as well.'

'A kept woman? Is that what you want to be?'

She nodded calmly. 'I'd rather be that than an exploited woman.'

Their talk went on for hours. She was immovable. Giles went through successive stages of outrage, disapproval, incomprehension, and finally sank to haggling.

'You know perfectly well I can't afford to keep a mistress. My salary isn't nearly enough.'

'Nonsense. There are lots of things you can cut back on.'

He was beaten. It turned out that he wanted her, feared losing her, and that this want and fear were stronger than that

156

impulse to direct and dominate which had always, up to now, been the strongest force in his life.

During their long talk, both drank glass after glass, and by the time a final position was reached they were both slightly drunk. It was too late to do anything with the evening except eat a scrappy meal out of a tin. As they ate, a sense of the exposed nerve of their new life came to both of them. Giles suddenly saw himself as the man who kept a mistress, an expensive and beautiful girl who laid out her life for his pleasure like an exotic garden. It was a new vision of himself and it intoxicated him. He couldn't afford it; after a few months, when his savings were gone, he would throw her out and live a quiet, industrious life, saving every penny. It couldn't last, but then why should it? And, by God, while he did have her ...

His glance became ravenous. Wiping his mouth, he stumbled across and took her in his arms. She guessed his thoughts, and they matched her own. A life based on this hard, throbbing enjoyment. To take everything she could get and in return to give pleasure, pleasure and more pleasure. Why not, why not? What were the alternatives?

First on the floor, then in bed, she squarely met his needs and her own. Afterwards, lying spent and relaxed, she suddenly thought of Leonard Smith. Which of the girls would have to do her job? Mousy Daphne? Excitable Jackie? Calm, married Phyllis? Suddenly she thought: they ought to interview me. I could tell them a thing or two. The thought shook her with laughter, which did not die away but grew and grew, so that her body quivered as if a rapid stream were running through her bones. Giles stirred uneasily; he had been almost asleep.

'Whass the joke?' he mumbled.

'Oh,' she gasped, 'just something I thought of. Oh, darling Giles,' she murmured, holding him tight and stroking his head, 'is the truth *always* funny?'

Death of the Hind Legs

When Dannie got back from seeing the bank manager his cigar was going like a furnace. That was always a bad sign.

'They won't help me, Elsie,' he said to me. 'They're on the other side. All they can think of is the money the site'll make when it's developed. They've sold me down the river. Judas Iscariots. They'll fold their arms and watch us go under.'

And he went into his office and banged the door.

I've often heard him go in like that, over the years, so I just got on with a bit of dusting. Well, I thought, the old place has its difficulties. But it'll last my time.

I used to be Number One dresser at the old Gaiety. You wouldn't believe me if I told you the stars I've helped into their costume, and fetched their Guinness and egg-flip, and the errands I've run for them. Yes, and the secrets I've kept. A lot of good stories'll die with me. Elsie, always as silent as the grave.

Dannie was a star himself in those days. A fine big man with a fine voice, and all the presence in the world. It's a big stage at the Gaiety, but he filled it all by himself. His songs were good and his patter was good. And now he was struggling on from week to week, managing the theatre. That was the easy part of it. Persuading the financing company to keep it going, that was real work. He was always going round to see them and arguing himself blue in the face. They didn't want to know. All they wanted was the balance-sheets to turn black instead of red, and they never did.

And me still there. No dressers now: but I cleaned out the dressing rooms, and made a cup of tea in between whiles, and listened while Dannie went on about his troubles. When he was in a good mood he'd say, 'You're my front of the house manager, Elsie,' he used to say. 'I'll pay you twelve pounds a week as soon as we turn the corner.' Other times he'd tell me it was all over and I was to go home and start packing for the work-house. But somehow, I never worried that much. I always came back to the thought: it'll last my time.

This particular day, it was lunch-time before I finished dusting out the dressing-rooms, and I only just had time to go across for a sandwich before the artistes started arriving. We were putting on three matinées a week during the school holidays. Dannie always relied on pantomime to pull them in. I think we were all glad when pantomime days came round. Most of the time it was travelling strip-shows, they were the only touring shows we could book, and there was no fun in having them about the place. Comedians who'd given up, and a low type of girl, for the most part. But it was all we had.

The pantomime was going quite well this year. Aladdin it was. The principal boy was a big, good-looking girl called Penny. They gave her some songs, to start off with, but they had to cut them out, she just couldn't sing in tune, though they kept her trying right up to the dress rehearsal. Then they gave her songs to her understudy, Muriel. There wasn't any love lost between those two. But Penny just couldn't sing in tune. She couldn't hear music.

I had my stout and sandwich and went back across the road. Mrs Whitaker from the box-office was away with her husband's bad back, *again*, so I had to go in the box-office and take the money. Not that there was much money to take. But a few trickled in, and the house didn't seem all that empty. I saw Dannie walking up and down in the foyer, looking out into the street as if he wanted to rush out and drag people in by force. His eyes were bloodshot. It's a shame, I thought. He ought to get away for a rest.

'How's it going, Elsie?' he asked, coming in to the box-office.

'There's about ninety in,' I said, adding it on a bit. 'Enough to play to.'

'Enough to play to!' he said with a nasty sarcastic laugh. 'Yes, that's the best we can hope for, isn't it? A few faces here and there among the empty seats.' And he stamped out.

I began to wonder if Leo and Walter had got in yet. They were the horse. I think both of them hated it about equally, it was such an insult to them to have to put on an animal's skin and trot about, when they both thought they were fine artists. Leo was Walter's nephew. He was about twenty-five, and Walter must have been, well, sixty. His face was like leather, very sad, and full of lines. But his eyes were deep and full of feeling – you had to keep looking at them when he was talking. He'd been a real actor, legit. Touring and repertory. He'd played with all the big names and in all the big theatres. Shakespeare? He knew reams of it by heart. A gentleman and a pro. But there was no work for him now and everything he earned from being the back legs of the horse he spent on drink. He was always on the short stuff.

Leo was good-looking in a flashy way. He had wavy hair and a profile. He didn't have any ambitions about legit work – what he wanted was to get into TV and then pictures, and make a lot of money and drive a big car, while he still had his looks. He hated the horse-skin even more than Walter did. 'What's it matter to him?' he used to say, right out in front of him, talking as if he wasn't there. 'He's on the way down. Waiting for the end. I've got my future in front of me – I don't want to waste time getting started.'

'At least you're the front legs, boy,' Walter said to him once. He had that real old actor's voice that could make anything sound dignified.

'So I should be,' said Leo. 'I've got good eyesight. It's hard enough even for me, squinting out of those ruddy eyeholes. If it was you in front, we'd fall into the orchestra-pit and break our necks the first five minutes.'

That wasn't right, talking to him like that. But Walter didn't really seem to notice anything. He just quietly bought himself another drink and sat staring into it.

Dannie took over from me at the box-office, to catch any late ones that might drift in, and I went backstage to see if I could help anybody. At heart, I was still a dresser, though nobody had anything for me to do nowadays, and as for the girls we got with the travelling shows, an undresser would be more like it.

I went round to the stage door and in there, blocking the passage with his big padded shoulders, was Leo, knocking for all he was worth on Penny's dressing-room door. She didn't have a dressing-room to herself, she shared it with Muriel and another girl, but I knew it was Penny he was after all right.

'Do you mind?' I said. 'I want to go and help the girls to get ready. First curtain in five minutes.'

He knocked again and said, 'She's hiding from me. She's just said something unforgivable and I want an apology.' His face was very red.

I called, 'It's me, Elsie. Will you open the door, please, Penny?'

There was a silence and then Penny's voice said, 'Not if he's there, that precious lady killer.'

'I want an apology for what you just said,' Leo put in loudly.

'Never mind him, dear,' I said. 'If he tries to interfere with you I'll go straight to Dannie and get him thrown out of the show.'

Leo laughed, right in my face.

'What year are you living in, Elsie? You know damned good and well Dannie can't throw anybody out of the show unless he throws the show after them. He just couldn't get a replacement.'

'For the front end of a horse?' I asked.

He went red again and said, 'Not even for that. And if you're so keen on the horse, why don't you try to find Walter? He's vanished somewhere.'

'What?' I said. That pulled me up short. 'You know Dannie made you responsible for getting him here. Didn't you bring him?'

'I brought him,' he said, shrugging. 'But he's gone again. Slipped out for another drink, most likely.'

'Well, you're on in fifteen minutes, the pair of you,' I said. 'Go and look for him and get into your costume, instead of hanging about here being a nuisance to everybody.'

'You look for him,' he said. 'I'm having an apology out of that bitch before she goes on.'

'Don't you talk like that,' I said, flaring up. 'If you want to stay in this business you'll learn to drop that kind of talk. Troupers may have their disagreements but they don't use that kind of language to one another.'

'They didn't in your day, you mean,' he said. 'They were all ladies and gentlemen, weren't they? Well, that's all gone, they're just blokes and birds now.' Then he turned and started hammering on the door again.

I was beside myself. I didn't know whether Walter had really got lost, or whether Leo was just saying so to get rid of me. I went along to their dressing-room: he wasn't there.

The horse's skin was lying over the back of a chair. It had a big printed papiermâché head, grinning. The head was upside down on the seat of the chair and it looked ghastly, somehow. Made me come over faint for a second. The only other person in there was Fred Tourtle, the comedian in the show. He was a very quiet man. It was as if he saved all his noise for the audience. Offstage you never got a word out of him. But he always had a nod and a smile for you. He had a big family at home.

'Fred,' I said. 'Where's Walter? He's on in ten minutes.'

'I've only just got here,' said Fred. He picked up the jacket of the baggy suit, with big checks, that he wore for his act. It seemed to me that he was looking at it the way Leo used to look at the horse's skin.

I ran out of the building. There was only one other place he could be. The 'Green Man'. And there he was, in the saloon, standing with one foot on the rail. It was towards closing-time and they were a bit full, so he hadn't been served yet. When I caught hold of his elbow he turned his face to me, and it gave me another shock, a much worse one this time.

'Hello, Elsie,' he said. 'Just having a pick-me-up before we go on.'

I can't describe his face. He looked like death, let it go at that.

'Walter, you shouldn't be here,' I said. 'You should be lying down.' 'In hospital,' I nearly added.

He shrugged. 'There's no point in lying down, Elsie, when the maddened populace are roaring for a sight of Billie, the panto-mime horse. And my ambitious young nephew is willing to shroud that profile of his in an equine mask. Miracles, Elsie, miracles. Who am I to stand in their way?'

He staggered slightly, not from drink, as far as I could see, but because he really hadn't any strength.

'Look, sit down,' I said. I accepted the situation. 'Go over there and sit down and I'll bring you a drink.'

He wandered off, and I rapped on the bar, very fiercely, and got served. I didn't care what they thought of me. I got him a double brandy – luckily, I'd got just enough money for it. I put just a splash of soda in it the way I knew he liked it, and took it over to him.

'If you're going on, Walter, we must be across in five minutes,' I said to him. 'But I'd just as soon go and tell Dannie you're under the weather.'

He shook his head, with his eyes closed. 'I'll go on,' he said.

All right, tell me I'm an old fool who can't see when a man ought to be in a hospital and when he ought to be capering about on a stage in front of a lot of bored school kids. I *knew* all right. But I thought of Dannie's face when he came back from the bank, and the half-empty house, and the horse's skin lying across the chair. And all Fred's kids at home. And may the good Lord forgive me, I thought, If he can get into the skin, he'll be all right.

We went across the road and in at the stage door. The show had started by then and Dannie was pacing up and down the corridor. He was furious, I could see that.

'That young bastard's out of the show,' he said. 'At the end of this week. Yes, your nephew, Walter,' he said, catching sight of Walter behind me.

Walter said nothing, so I said, 'What's he been doing?'

'Doing?' Dannie snorted. 'He broke the most sacred rule in the business. Quarrelled with another artiste and upset her just as she was going on.'

I might have known. But what could I have done? I had to go across and fetch Walter, or he'd still have been in the 'Green Man' now.

'He took advantage of the fact that he wasn't onstage till ten minutes after Penny,' Dannie went on. 'He was lurking out here when she and the others came out for the opening number.'

'And did what?' I said. 'Walter, you'd better get into costume.'

'He – he *molested* her in some way,' said Dannie. 'I wasn't actually on the spot myself. But she slapped his face, I know that. And by the time I got here, she was just going onstage. Shaking, she was, with nerves and annoyance. *Shaking*. That's a fine way to start a show.'

Walter had gone off to get togged up.

'Where's Leo now?' I asked.

'Waiting for Walter,' said Dannie. 'I tell you, we're in trouble. The show's collapsing round our ears, Elsie.'

'Things have been bad before,' I said, to comfort him.

'Not *this* bad. Listen, Elsie, I'll tell you something. It's all up. They're closing us down. They want us to stop at the end of this week. Saturday night'll be the last show. Then the demolition starts on Monday.'

'You must be joking,' I said.

'Does it sound like a joke?'

'But what about advance bookings?' I said, fighting for breath. Dannie laughed, almost as if it was really funny. 'Are you raving mad, Elsie? We haven't got any advance bookings. Haven't had any since Boxing Day. No, we stop on Saturday. I'm not telling the others, but I'm telling you, so you can pack for the workhouse.'

I just stood there. All I could think, in that moment, was that I understood why Dannie had sacked Leo. Told him to finish on Saturday. If we were all finishing on Saturday, he could afford to do it, and it relieved his feelings.

'They've had one of these big offers for the site,' said Dannie. He got out a cigar and stood looking at it, as if he was too unhappy even to make up his mind to light it. 'They're all going to be rich. Inside a month, nobody'll even remember that the Gaiety was here. And you and I'll be ghosts, Elsie.'

'Well,' I said. 'I'd better get Leo and Walter onstage.' And I walked off down the corridor.

The horse was standing there when I knocked on the door and went in. So at least I didn't have to look at Leo's expression. I caught sight of one of his eyes, glaring out of the horse's eyehole on that side, and it was enough to be going on with.

'How's Walter in there?' I asked the horse's head.

'Never better, dear,' came Walter's voice from the middle somewhere. It was a bit ghostly, but it was still the same rich old actor's voice as ever, and it did me good.

'Walter's all right,' said the horse's head. 'It's me that's got something to complain about. No bird slaps me and gets away with it.'

'Listen, try to think of the show for a bit,' I said. 'You're on in half a minute. Keep your mind on what you're doing.'

'I know what I'm doing,' Leo's voice said very coldly. I had a horrible feeling that he'd made up some nasty little scheme to get revenge on Penny. And then I thought, Oh, well! Four more shows and that's our lot – and I'm worrying!

The bell rang and the horse walked down to the wings, waited for cue, and went on. I stood there with my mouth all dry. I felt dead inside. Pack for the workhouse! Well, why not?

Then Dannie came and stood beside me and started peering on to the stage.

'What's that young devil doing?' he muttered between his teeth. He rubbed his eyes, as if he couldn't believe what he was seeing, and stared again. 'My God!' he said. 'He's attacking her!'

I twisted round and looked past him on to the stage. In this scene, Penny did a short comic routine with the horse. She was supposed to be leaving home to seek her fortune or something, and the horse belonged to the Widow Twankey, and they had this bit of fooling about before Aladdin took his leave. Most of the horse's other business was with Fred, of course, but this little bit had been added to give the horse something more to do. Well, as I stood in the wings and stared past Dannie, I saw what it was that was making him so amazed. The horse had got Penny into a corner of the stage and was sort of crowding her, yes, really pushing against her. Penny was backing and circling away, and there was a bit of laughter coming from the audience, but the laughter was uneasy somehow, as if they weren't quite sure whether it was meant to be funny.

I saw it all in a flash, Leo was mad with rage, yes, mad. I could imagine the sort of things he was saying to Penny, quietly, under his breath, and he was so blind with fury that he was barging and bumping her almost without knowing it. The horse was moving in a peculiar way and I could tell that Walter was troubled about what was going on, and was trying to hang back and restrain Leo.

'My Christ,' said Dannie. 'Next thing, they'll be struggling with one another inside the bloody skin.'

He leant against the woodwork, really faint. It was the first time in all the years I'd seen him like this, not knowing what on earth to do.

'You'll have to bring the curtain down if this goes on,' I said to him. 'Bring the curtain down and start the scene again.'

'We can't do that,' he was just beginning to say – I could read his mind – but he hadn't got any further than 'can't' when we both stiffened and held our breath. Something very strange was happening to the horse. It was canting over on its side, then it was down, kicking a few times, then the rear half wasn't kicking any more. Leo was trying to get up, but Walter's half just lay there on the stage.

'No, my God, no!' said Dannie in a terrible croaking voice. 'This had to happen today! Walter's fainted!'

The truth is I knew straight away Walter hadn't fainted, he'd died. I was the only person who knew that Leo was struggling to move that skin with a dead man in there with him, and for a few minutes I stood there hugging that knowledge to myself like a cold, wet rope tied round my chest.

'Curtain!' Dannie shouted, not caring whether the audience heard him or not. The stage-hands had it down in a second, and we all ran onstage to do what we could. As we did so, Penny hurried off. She brushed right by me, looking straight ahead, and her face was absolutely dead white.

The skin unzipped down the back; the men couldn't do it themselves, they had to have someone else to help them. It must have been Fred who'd fastened it for them before they came on, and now he was there again, kneeling by the sprawling shape of the horse and pulling away at the zip. It came open, and Leo snatched the horse's head off and scrambled out.

'What goes on?' he said, very shaken.

'I think we might ask you that,' said Dannie, grimly. 'But let's get Walter out before we start quarrelling. And get one of the girls out in front to tell them it's a technical hitch. Say the curtain will go up again in five minutes.'

'But how can we –' someone started.

'Five minutes!' Dannie hissed in that way he has, when his blood is up and nobody tries to argue with him. One of the girls went round to the front of the curtain and we heard her speaking to the audience, soothing them and jollying them along. The rest of us got Walter out of the skin and carried him backstage. Surely, I thought, now that they've picked him up they'll *see* he's dead. But they didn't. It wasn't until he was on the sofa in Dannie's office, and everyone stood back to look at him, that they got a proper sight of his face. I won't go into details. But it wasn't the face of a living man.

I don't know who was upset the most. Dannie was knocked all of a heap. Coming on top of what he'd had to face that day, it must have seemed to him like the end of the world. But Leo was just as badly hit. He fell on his knees by the side of the body and started crying like a child.

Everybody else was silent, trying not to listen to Leo's crying, and in the end Dannie looked round for me and said, 'Get the doctor, Elsie.'

'Wouldn't it be quicker to ask if there's one in the house?' one of the girls asked. Dannie turned his face towards her, and it had hardly any more life in it than Walter's.

'Quick?' he said. 'Why should we be quick?'

I knew he was beaten. Forty years I'd known him, and this was his moment of defeat. Perhaps it comes to all of us, but somehow I'd never looked to see it come to him.

Then, suddenly, Leo got up off his knees.

'Dannie,' he said, 'let's go on with the show.'

The tears were still running down his face and everybody just thought he had gone mad. But I didn't. I guessed what he was feeling.

'Go on with the show?' Dannie rounded on him. 'That's fine, coming from you. If you hadn't been so – ' he ended with a wave of his hand. It was too much to put into words.

'Look,' said Leo. 'You told that girl to say the curtain would be raised again in five minutes.'

'That's just routine,' said Dannie tiredly. 'Stops 'em from thinking there's a fire. If you didn't say that they'd stampede for the entrance and tear each other to pieces getting out. That curtain'll never go up again.'

'Dannie, *please*,' said Leo. 'Walter's dead. It can't hurt him now if we go on. It's what he'd have wanted.'

'You don't understand,' said Dannie. He looked round help-lessly, as if all he wanted was for the theatre and all of us to disappear in a twinkling, and leave him alone in a desert where he wouldn't have to speak to anybody. 'You don't understand. The game's up anyway. They've closed us down.'

'Who have?' said Fred.

'The backers,' said Dannie. 'The people that own the place. The site's going to be used for office buildings. The Gaiety comes down on Monday. Nobody knows yet. But that's it.'

At that moment Penny came in. She'd been in her dressing-room by herself, having a good cry or something. But she was quite composed now, and the shock and strain made her face seem more fine-drawn, and really, more beautiful. She'd heard what Dannie said about the place coming down.

'That's the end,' she said. 'Too late for regrets now.'

'Penny,' said Leo. He went up to her. 'I want to say I'm sorry.'

'It doesn't matter.'

'I'll never act like that to anyone again. I feel terrible about it.'

'It doesn't matter. Not now,' she said.

Then one of the stage-hands came in. One of the two stage-hands.

'Shall we get the curtain up, Dannie?' he said. 'They're getting impatient.' It was clear he didn't know about Walter. Then he caught sight of him lying on the sofa. 'My God,' he said.

'Yes, get it up,' said Leo. He whirled round on Dannie. 'You must let us go on. Do it for Walter's sake.'

'So you're a sentimental fool as well as everything else,' said Dannie.

I thought that had settled it, but Penny spoke.

'Let's do it, Dannie,' she said. 'Walter was a trouper. He wouldn't have wanted us to sit about and moan about him. And turn an audience away. They've come to see the show, we've taken their money. I don't mind going on if no one else does.'

'Till Saturday night?' put in Fred, as if he was thinking aloud.

'Yes, till Saturday night,' said Penny. 'If the Gaiety's coming down we might as well play till the wreckers come.'

'But who,' Dannie began, and stopped. He looked at Leo for a moment, without any expression, then suddenly laughed very loudly. 'You do mean me, don't you?'

'Why not?' said Leo. 'You rehearsed us. You know all the routines.'

The pair of them looked at the horse's skin. It seemed to look back at them.

'Well,' said Dannie, 'if it's good enough for a fine artist like Walter, it's good enough for me.' He picked it up. 'Get the curtain up. We'll start the scene again. And Elsie,' he said to me, 'don't go. You'll have to zip us into this thing.'

My brain just wasn't working. All I could do was move about like a machine, doing what I was told. But one thought of my own I did have. I couldn't bear to see Walter lying there, not even covered up. I went and found a blanket and put it over him. Then I zipped Leo and Dannie into the horse.

The curtain went up, they started again at the beginning of that scene, and the show ran on rails right through to the finale. I didn't see any of it, because I was ringing up various undertakers to get Walter taken away. It took me a long time to find one, but I persevered. I knew he lived in a bed-sitter somewhere, and I was quite certain the landlady wouldn't want him coming home in that condition. And also, I was waiting for the doctor to arrive. He must have been busy, because he didn't come for over two hours, by which time the show was finishing. I could hear the final chorus backstage.

'Where is the deceased?' he asked me abruptly. He was a doctor of the old school, with that hoity-toity manner they all used to have, but only the older ones have now.

'In the office,' I said.

The doctor went in and I could see him, through the half-open door, take the blanket off and give Walter a quick once-over. Heart failure, of course. He went over to the desk to fill the form up, and at that moment Leo and Dannie came along the corridor in the horse's skin.

'Get us out of this thing, Elsie,' said Leo's voice.

'All right,' I said. 'But Dannie's wanted in the office.'

Without hesitating, Leo turned and marched into the office, with Dannie bringing up the rear. The doctor, hearing someone come in, straightened up from the desk and looked round. I could see it gave him a bit of a shock to see the horse standing there. He probably hadn't been to a pantomime in recent years.

'Who are you?' he said. A silly question, I suppose, but he had to say something.

'I'm the manager,' said Dannie's voice from somewhere amidships.

'And I'm the nephew,' Leo added from the horse's head.

The doctor got round to the other side of the desk.

'Is this a madhouse? I come here to sign a certificate of death and I'm met by this – this – '

'Wait, please,' said Dannie's voice. 'I'll be with you straight away. About turn, Leo.' And the horse swung round and cantered off to the dressing-room.

Tut-tutting to himself, the doctor put back the blanket over Walter and stood waiting. He caught sight of me watching him from the corridor and barked. 'It's disgraceful – this nonsense! Disgraceful!'

'Some people do die at work, you know,' I said.

'Work? What was he doing?'

'He was in the horse,' I said.

The doctor started violently. His nerves were shaken, and it must have seemed to him that the damned horse was everywhere.

'Elsie!' came a shout from down the passage.

'Oh!' I exclaimed. 'I forgot. Coming!' And I rushed off to unzip them.

Leo stepped out first. 'Congratulations, Dannie,' he said, wiping the sweat off his face with a paper handkerchief. 'You did fine. Specially the dance. We got out of step, but that only made it funnier.'

Dannie smiled and reached for his jacket. 'Get some rest,' he said, moving to the door. 'The second house begins in an hour. Have you made the tea, Elsie?'

'It's drawing,' I said. Dannie always had a pot of tea and a pork pie after a matinée.

He went off to cope with the doctor, and Leo sank down on a chair, looking thoughtful.

'Do you think I'm unnatural, Elsie?' he asked me suddenly.

'Some people would,' I said.

'Yes, but do you?' he pressed.

I thought for a moment. 'No,' I said. 'Those people paid to be entertained and it's not their fault Walter died. And that's how Walter would have seen it.'

'Even when it's all over anyway? when the theatre's coming down?'

'All the more reason,' I said. 'Penny was right.'

'She was marvellous this afternoon, Elsie,' said Leo. His eyes were shining as he thought of her. 'Just *marvellous*. She could have played – *anywhere*. In any theatre in the world.' And he took himself off, humming a tune.

It's like that, is it? I thought. And hanging was too good for her a couple of hours ago. Well, young people are funny. Their world can change in a moment.

Dannie came back from seeing the doctor off the premises. 'Tea, Elsie,' he said, rubbing his hands together as he did when he was pleased. I could see the doctor hadn't been able to come it over *him*. 'And then, as soon as you've made it, please tell everyone I want to see them for a moment. We'll assemble onstage in ten minutes.'

I did as he said. The whole company, stage-hands and all, were waiting onstage for him when he'd finished his cup of tea. They were all wearing hats and coats, ready for off. There isn't much time between performances, when the second house is at seven-thirty by kind permission of the bus companies.

'All right, everybody,' said Dannie. 'You'll have heard by now. First, that Walter died during the performance today. He was a trouper and a gentleman, he was worth far better things than to be the back legs of a horse, but he never complained, and may he rest in the peace he deserves. Second, we're folding. The owners have gone behind my back and sold the place, and the new people are in such a hurry to start making money that we're closing on Saturday night and the old Gaiety's going to be knocked down on Monday morning. That means four more performances. It gives you a little time to look round for new jobs, those of you who'll be able to find 'em, and I know as well as anyone that not all of you will. You younger ones will be all right, but even for you there'll probably be some waiting and some hungry times. As for me, it's the end of the line. I don't know what I'll do. But I'll have plenty of time to think about it and I expect I'll come up with something. But meanwhile, I know one thing. Till midnight on Saturday, I'm still the manager of the Gaiety Theatre. We've got four more performances, and I want to make them the very best we can do. Let's stay together till then. After the way you've been let down, I couldn't blame anyone who just walked out of the show tonight. But somehow, I don't think you will.'

'No, Dannie, we won't,' said Penny, so loudly that her voice went ringing out over the rows of empty seats. I noticed Leo's arm steal round her waist. She didn't make any effort to pull away, either.

'And one more thing,' said Dannie. 'We're having a wake for Walter, Saturday night, after the show. We'll have a party onstage, and if there's a few quid left in the kitty it can all go on food and drink. Bring your friends. Let's have the house well papered for that last show – I want to see every seat filled. We'll put on a performance they'll never forget and at the end of it we'll invite our friends and have a party. In honour of Walter and – in memory of the Gaiety.'

'Thanks, Dannie,' said Leo's voice, so quietly that I wondered if Dannie heard.

'That's all,' said Dannie shortly. 'Back here at seven. Everybody go and relax a bit. Eat and drink.'

They trooped off, rather silently. Nobody seemed to want to hang about. The idea of a party on the Saturday night had gone down well with them all, but Saturday night seemed a long time. Four more shows to get through, with the shadow of the chopper at the end of it.

I went into Dannie's office to clear away his tea-things. I found him just putting the telephone receiver down.

'That's settled, then, Elsie,' he said. 'Walter's to be buried on Saturday morning.'

And the Gaiety's to be murdered on Monday, I thought. My face must have shown the mood I was in, because Dannie came round the desk and put his arm round my shoulders.

'I know, Elsie, I know,' he said. 'But let's go down with our guns firing, shall we?'

'Guns, is it?' I said. 'D'you know what I'm going to do, when those offices go up? I'm going to get a job cleaning them. Then there'll always be a little bit of the Gaiety here.'

We all looked at each other and then we laughed. At that moment Leo put his head in at the door.

'Same arrangements for tonight, Dannie?' he asked. 'Horse-wise, I mean?'

'Same arrangements,' said Dannie. 'I can't start looking for a new pair of hind legs at this stage of the game. I shall finish my career in ... comedy.' And he gave a self-satisfied nod.

Walter was buried on the Saturday morning, in a windy churchyard surrounded by mean little houses. The Reverend spouted it all out in about ten minutes flat, but there was Dannie to lend dignity to the scene, and Leo and Penny came, and one or two others from the company. I brought up the rear. In spite of the dismal graveyard and the cold wind, it was rather a happy occasion for me, because I was watching Penny and Leo and the happiness was coming off them like electricity. Things must have been moving between them pretty fast, and whatever had happened, it had certainly changed them. Penny was always a fine, good-looking girl, but now her eyes had lost a certain wary look that had always haunted them. She looked trusting, open. And Leo's face had changed altogether. He'd lost that pushing, jeering, hard look he used to have. And he held himself more easily.

As a matter of fact, I might say nearly as much for everyone in the company. Now that the Gaiety was under sentence of death, they were throwing themselves into the show like never before. Dannie in particular. He worked at that hind legs business *all the time*. He and Leo used to rehearse, yes, actually rehearse when they had only three more shows to do, then two, then one. Trying out bits of new business. The show got longer by about ten minutes each time, as the horse had more to do. And Dannie was thriving on it. He used to climb out of that skin with sweat absolutely running down his face. 'Taking pounds off, Elsie,' he'd say to me. 'It's doing me the world of good. If I'd known what good exercise this was, I'd have taken it up years ago.' 'You be careful you don't get a cardiac,' I'd tell him.

Some people, I know, would put it down to wanting to forget his troubles. When he was capering about with Leo in the skin he couldn't be worrying about his future or shedding tears over the Gaiety. But I understood Dannie better. It was his salute to the life he'd lived, and to the Gaiety, and to Walter.

Well, Saturday night came and it was the last time round. The place was papered to the ceiling. Everyone in the company had invited about twenty of their friends. It all went with a swing from the start. In fact I've never seen a show like it. Dannie and Leo practically took over the show – the horse was onstage almost all the time. And Fred! He threw away the script and created his part over again from scratch. His ad-libbing was wonderful, he was having the audience in fits and the people onstage with him too, so that quite a number of times they couldn't go on for laughing. And yet, I was glad to see, he didn't use any blue gags. It was still a family show, there were kids in the audience, and as a family man he respected that. As a matter of fact his own kids were there, all six or eight or however many there were. I stood in the wings and watched Fred, giving his all. I knew he'd never work again. Like me, he'd probably thought it would last his time, and like me he'd been wrong. He was too old and too traditional to make a name for himself on television, and as for theatres like the Gaiety, there just weren't any more, we were about the last. A bit of seasonal work on a pier in summer was the best he could hope for, and with a family that size it would be hopeless. He'd be driving a van or something; after thirty years in show business, he had no future. And if I knew all this, it was a safe bet that Fred knew it too. But there he was, giving a really inspired performance, working as hard as any young comic out to grab his chances.

Then the final chorus was sung, the curtain came down and went up a few times for applause, and it was over. Just the party, a few drinks, a few laughs, and then we'd take our hats and coats out and the bulldozers could start any time they pleased. Everybody flooded on to the stage as soon as they'd got out of their costumes, and I was working hard to get all the bottles and glasses and pies and sandwiches laid out on tables. Dannie had been as good as his word: the kitty had been cleaned out and everything had gone on good fare, liquid and solid.

Among the crowd there were lots of people I'd never seen before, naturally, what with all the friends that had been invited, but my eye was caught by two in particular. They were with Leo, and the whisper went round that they were relatives of Walter's. They looked very out of place. Well dressed in a stiff, expensive way. Not aristocratic, nothing like that, but well-heeled business, very particular as to who they mixed with, very certain that they weren't going to give any points away in the social game. Poor old Walter must have been a black sheep.

I felt a bit sorry for them, at first. Leo quite clearly thought that he'd done his duty by getting them into the building and inviting them to the party. He introduced them to Dannie and then moved off to concentrate on Penny. Naturally, Dannie didn't want to get trapped with them either, so he just poured them out a drink each, made a few suitable remarks, smiled at them, and left them alone. They were standing together at the edge of the stage, he in his neatly-pressed business suit, she in a twin set and pearls, breathing money and respectability and – I saw when I went close up to them – disapproval.

To make conversation I said, 'I didn't see you at Walter's funeral.'

'We got held up in traffic,' said the man, 'driving down from Surbiton.'

'The traffic was terrible,' said his wife. 'It took us an hour longer than we expected, and that meant the funeral was over when we got here. But we visited the grave.'

'Yes,' the husband echoed, 'we visited the grave.'

Then it suddenly seemed to dawn on both of them that they were talking to somebody who hadn't been introduced, and they both shrank away. One look at me and they didn't *want* to be introduced.

'I'm the dresser,' I said, giving myself back my old style for a moment. Why not, on a night like this? Another few hours and there wouldn't be a Gaiety at all, and nobody would ever know the difference again. 'Yes, the dresser, I am. I knew Walter very well, naturally.'

'Poor Walter,' said the woman, and suddenly I could see that her tight little face was made, originally, in the same mould as Walter's. This must be the sister. 'Poor Walter,' she said again, with pity and disgust mixed about equally in her voice. 'Fancy ... dying among people like this!'

Following her eyes, I looked round at the company and their friends. Some were singing, some were telling jokes, giving imitations, laughing. You wouldn't have thought they had a care in the world.

'I'm sixty-two,' I said to this woman. 'I'll die a lot sooner than you will. And I'd like you to know that these people are probably a lot better than the people you'll die among.'

'*Better?*' she said, recoiling.

'More to like in them,' I said.

The man gave me a cold look and said, 'You don't understand. Walter had a wonderful career once. And to die like that – in a horse's skin at a pantomime – '

'Never mind about the horse's skin, for a moment,' I said. 'Let's just say that he died entertaining the public. And perhaps entertaining them is just as much worth doing as – screwing money out of them.'

They were angry now. They both turned their eyes on me, like two goldfish in a bowl.

'And while I'm on the subject of money,' I said, 'I wouldn't mind betting that if Walter had earned five hundred pounds a week by prancing about in that skin, you wouldn't have thought it was a come-down at all.'

'Come on, Edith,' the man said suddenly. He put his drink down, half-emptied. 'We're wasting our time here.' And without a glance at me or a word of farewell to anyone, they walked off.

I was glad they'd gone, because they seemed to me, when I looked at them closely, to be a part of that world that had tried so long to destroy the Gaiety, to crunch up its old bones for money. Well, it was done, they had succeeded. But in these last few hours I felt that people from that world had no business here, and I knew Walter would have felt the same.

From the other side of the stage I could hear Fred begin to tell one of his stories. Just to hear his voice made me feel wonderful. So I filled my glass and went over to join in the laughter.